Takedown

E. M. J. Benjamin

"And Jacob was left alone; and a man wrestled with him until the breaking of the day."

Genesis 32:24

CHAPTER 1

I hate wrestling! What a stupid sport! I'm pacing back and forth, jumping up and down, trying to break a sweat, but I'm so nervous nothing's happening. I can't believe I'm this hyper. I'm a wreck, for cryin' out loud. Here I am: a senior, two-time state qualifier, and the guy I'm going up against isn't that good. I ought to be thinking how I'm going to kick his butt. But no. My body has turned to ice.

Coach Lindy always says, "You're not warmed up enough, Jake. You should be dripping wet before you go out on the mat." Some joke. I'm a mass of frozen neurons. I'm lucky I can make myself move at all.

I'm always this way before a match. Always.

I hate this sport.

The 140-pounders are about to start. Our guy, Marcus, takes off his lucky earring, hands it to Coach, and snaps his headgear in place. Marcus is good, so his match won't last long – and then I'll be on the mat, with Dad and my brother Chopper watching from the stands and expecting me to win. Fortunately my girlfriend Callie is at chorus tonight and won't have to see. I try to swallow but there's no spit in my mouth, not a drop. I have this to look forward to the whole season. And it's only the beginning.

Our freshman 103-pounder, Polson, catches my eye and gives me thumbs-up. He's a feisty little fellow but doesn't know much yet. Half an hour ago he got pinned in the first period. Coach says, "If you're lucky, Pole, you won't suck at the end of the year. You'll progress from super-sorry to sorry. If you work hard and you're lucky." Pole's watching me and thinking, "There's Jake, a real veteran, about to go out there and take care of business. There's not a doubt in his mind."

Don't I wish. Having the flu for the past two weeks hasn't helped. I'm better, but not a hundred percent. I missed a lot of practice. I'm not even in shape.

In the center of the gym, Marcus immediately rolls his guy into a pinning combination. Marcus ought to win most of the time this season, but he's my workout partner and I know I'm better than he is. So why doesn't he ever get scared? He can tell a joke ten seconds before he has to wrestle, like there's nothing else on his mind. He's so cool it drives me crazy.

"It's only natural, man. Watch any sport on TV. You won't see any black guys get nervous. Just you skinny white guys."

"Real helpful, Marcus."

"Not your fault, Jake. It's in the blood."

Right.

In front of us, Marcus bears down on his opponent's chest and pushes the guy's shoulders toward the mat. The kid grunts, then flattens and goes limp. He can't even fight it out until second period. The ref slaps the mat to signal the pin. It's over. I'm going to be out there quicker than I thought.

Next thing I know, I'm shaking hands with a blond kid a little taller than I am, and the ref is blowing the whistle for us to start. I don't want to be here, but it's too late.

My heart's beating so hard I'm sure the kid can hear it. I psyche myself up by telling myself the second I get my hands on his legs, he's history.

I shoot a low single – too quick, without setting it up right, and the blond guy sprawls away from me. Mom, who hates to watch wrestling because she's afraid I'll get hurt, says the word *shoot* reminds her of guns and battles. But all it means is crouching low and lunging toward the guy's ankles so you knock him off balance and get control.

The idea is always to get control.

That first out-of-bounds helps me relax. I begin to focus. I start to think, "Hey, this is my turf and nobody comes here and pushes me around." When the whistle blows again, I'm wary. We circle a little. I concentrate on the ankles. Come on buddy, take a step forward. Right into my trap.

When I shoot, I get in deep, hit him hard, but he doesn't go down. My ear connects with something so solid that for a second I see black dots in front of my eyes. What did I hit? I've done that move a hundred times and never gotten jolted like that before. The blond guy grabs his leg and yelps. The ref blows the whistle to stop it.

It takes us both a minute to recover.

After that my mind is fuzzy from the blow, but maybe that's good because it makes me operate on instinct. As Coach Lindy always says, you can't think and wrestle at the same time. If you're busy analyzing the move you're going to try next, chances are you won't get it. "Don't try to be Einstein," Coach likes to say. "If you want to be Einstein, join the math team."

A second later I shoot and finally get the first takedown. The two points don't seal the victory by a long shot, but suddenly I feel better. The way he can't hold me off, I know I can take him down twenty times. He knows it, too. His mindset is going from "I hope I'm going to win" to "I hope I don't get pinned." I know because I've been there. I let him go. He gets a point for the escape, but now I'm ready for him. I shoot. Take him down. Two points. I can do this all day.

By the end of second period, I'm ahead ten to five. I remember now why Pole thinks I'm so good. When I was his age, I could be up by seven with one minute left in the match, and I'd still be worried. Now I know the guy is tiring. I know exactly what he's got left. My ear's still buzzing from hitting it, but I feel strong and sure.

By third period my mind is wandering to the pizza I'm going to eat later. Don't get me wrong, it's not in the center of my mind, not distracting me from anything, but it's there. This might sound weird, but thinking about food is how I know I'm really on my game. Last night I had to run three miles because I left practice two pounds heavy. Today all I ate before weigh-ins was half a peanut butter sandwich, and after weigh-ins another half sandwich and a banana. But when this is over, I'm eating pizza, and lots of it.

Pretty soon my body's doing what it's supposed to without my mind getting in the way. I hit an arm bar – something I'm not usually good at – and turn the guy to his back. I bear down. With twenty seconds left in the period, the ref slaps the mat for a pin. I get my hand raised in victory, I tell my opponent the traditional, "good match" and run back to get the high fives from my teammates. I love this sport!

After pulling off my headgear, I take a seat on the bench beside Marcus, who smiles and says, "What took you so long?" Across the gym in the bleachers, Dad gives me a thumbs-up sign and Chopper raises his fists and punches the air.

The rest of the team is thinking, Jake took care of business like he always does. Me, I'm wondering why I was ever so worried. I'm debating what kind of pizza to order. I have no clue about the cyclone already brewing in my brain, no clue my life's about to do a one-eighty.

All I'm thinking about is that extra cheese.

CHAPTER 2

An hour later we're sitting in Lefty's Pizza – Dad, Chopper, Marcus, and me. Dad works evenings and nights at Palisades Industries, but when I have a match he either makes sure he's on the graveyard shift or else takes off. Chopper says Dad is trying to be supportive now that Mom has made her Big Career Move, but that's not it. Dad's been to every home meet since I was a freshman. He loves the idea that one of his sons is on any kind of varsity team. The only sport Chopper loves is surfing the Internet. He's fourteen years old and weighs 97 pounds, not because he's naturally skinny but because when he gets interested in something online, he forgets to eat.

Right now he's chowing down. So are Marcus and I, though I feel a little guilty because I have to make weight again later this week. It's amazing how good a pizza tastes when you've been starving all day. Only thing is, for some reason the cheese smells kind of gross tonight. Tastes all right, just smells bad. Which is weird, because Lefty's pizza is the best.

Marcus puts another slice on his plate. It's amazing he's eaten anything at all, given that he's been jabbering nonstop since we got here and shows no sign of letting up. Having a captive audience makes Marcus a happy man. Especially if he's also coming off a win and filling his belly.

No kidding: above all else, Marcus loves attention.

He will do anything to get it. Anything. Couple of years ago he pulled a drowning kid out of a swimming pool, and he still carries the picture from the paper around in his wallet. Marcus the hero. But he gets the same kick from a stunt he pulled last summer when he stole ten bucks from a weasely kid at wrestling camp. After the kid made a big fuss, he taped the money to the guy's door along with a note about his lack of intelligence and wrestling skills. Everybody knew Marcus was guilty, but nobody could prove it. He loved it. Lived on the gossip the rest of the week. Talks about it all the time.

"Man, if only Brunson didn't have to wait 'til football's over to wrestle," he says through a mouthful of pizza. "We'd kick butt." Brunson is our heavyweight, but also a first-string offensive lineman who won't be on the mats until the football season ends.

"I think that's why a lot of states start their wrestling season in December instead of November like we do," Chopper says.

"Yeah?" Marcus acts interested but isn't really listening. He shakes his head and arranges his face into a dramatic, mournful expression. "Man, I still wish Mama hadn't made me promise not to go out for football. I think I could of done it."

"You're small for football," Dad says. "You and Jake both."

"Yeah, and sometimes you have to listen to Mama." I give him an elbow. Marcus likes pointing out how concerned his mother is for him, especially when she's not around. She missed the meet tonight because she has a new boyfriend. We won't see much of her until she gets tired of him. Now that our own Mom spends her weekdays traveling around the state for the bank, Chopper and I can sympathize.

"Take it from a man who played freshman football," I tell Marcus as I raise a slice of pizza to my mouth. "Unless you're a major beefer, they're not interested in you. You spend most of your time chewing on your mouthpiece and listening to them cuss at you. How'd your mother like to know they call you a piece of horseshit?"

The rotten-cheese smell hits me just as I'm about to chomp down on the pizza. I put it back on the plate.

"You guys are just jealous," Chopper says. "You wish you played football because then the babes would be after you and you'd get your picture in the paper. Nobody cares about wrestling except wrestlers." Doink that he is, sometimes Chopper surprises you.

He pushes his glasses up on the little bump that passes for his nose. "Your ear is all swollen," he tells me.

"Duh. I did my famous low single into that blond kid's shin."

"Just a point of information."

I finger my cauliflower ear. It started getting gnarled and bumpy about a year ago when I first perfected my shot. The hallmark of a good low-single man. Although it's sore and sensitive at the moment, I wouldn't trade it.

"Aren't you going to finish eating, Jake?" Dad asks.

"Naw, I'm full." It's like someone has put my nose into high gear. Cheese stinks. It plain stinks. I wonder why I never noticed before.

"Then let's roll," Dad says.

Marcus pulls some money out of his pocket, but Dad waves it away. "You know what, Marcus? I'm surprised you're still wishing you'd played football. Football is the past. Senior year is the time to think about the future."

Uh-oh, I think. He's going into Lecture Mode.

"What you might think about," he tells Marcus the minute we get in the car, "is joining the military." He catches Marcus' eye in the rearview mirror. "It would get you out of here. Best thing that could happen to you."

I kick Dad in the leg, but he pays no attention. Dad wants to rescue Marcus from the perils of the black ghetto. Marcus's older brother is in jail. His mother's new boyfriend is probably a drug dealer. Marcus will be lucky if the boyfriend doesn't teach him his trade. He'll be lucky if his mother comes to a couple of matches. Otherwise, look out. Chopper once noted that Marcus never lost a match or caused trouble when his mother was in the stands, and when I thought about it, he was right.

The reason Dad likes taking Marcus out to eat with us is because, if our family is confused lately with Mom away, Marcus's family is disaster. Disaster cubed. The question of the evening is: can Marcus be saved?

"Getting in the service isn't as easy as it once was," Dad says. "But you're a smart guy, you could do it."

I nudge Dad again, and again he ignores me. Ever since his four years in the Marines before I was born, he's always worn his hair so short people think he made it his career. He views military service as a cure-all for confused young men everywhere. He gives me and Chopper every Marine Corps T-shirt he can get his hands on. Gloats about the Navy ROTC scholarship I've been offered. Lobbies for me to take the Marine option. "Even if you only stay in the required four years after college," he tells me, "it will focus you. Help you grow up." Now he's devising a similar plan for Marcus. If he thought about it for a second, he'd shut up.

We drop Marcus off on the corner by the Booker T. Washington housing project. Rows of brick duplexes line the street, with barren yards behind thcm and clotheslines strung across. If you drive through Booker T. in the daytime, it looks abandoned. At night people huddle in all the doorways and sit on the stoops, primarily scary-looking unemployed men who secretly live with the welfare women who rent the houses. Booker T. is known for its regular stabbings and fist fights, its occasional shooting. Dad would take Marcus to his door but Marcus says he'll walk. The truth is, Marcus is afraid for us. You never know what might happen if we drove in, dropped him off, and then tried to get out again, a car full of white guys.

The only white person I know who drives through Booker T. at night is Coach Lindy. After away meets, when he's taking the project kids home because none of them have cars, nobody hassles him at all. Everybody waves and says, "How ya doin, man?" and Coach waves back. Coach is the guy who takes a couple of Booker T. kids as far as the state tournament every year. The brothers value him. When you're white like me, driving through Booker T. at two in the morning under Coach's protection makes you feel invincible.

After Marcus disappears, as Dad revs the engine and speeds away, I notice the smell of pizza cheese again. It makes no sense. But the whole car reeks of it. I open the window.

"You shouldn't feed Marcus all that military crap," I tell Dad, irritated as much by the odor as by Dad's comments. "The military isn't going to take Marcus."

"Why not?"

"Because he brought that stun gun to school last

spring," Chopper puts in. This is the kind of information Chopper retains. "They sent him to the Alternative School. Don't you remember?"

"He made a mistake, but he paid for it," Dad says. "There's no reason he can't go on with his life."

"When you get arrested and suspended for the rest of the semester, the military doesn't take kindly to you," I note.

"I'm sure they look at the rest of your record."

"You're the one who says it's not like it used to be, when you got the choice of going to jail or going into the Marines. You're the one who says they don't take you anymore if you're a troublemaker. Marcus has been in and out of the Alternative School three times already." I don't know why I'm this annoyed, but I am. My head is so fuzzy from the musky smell of cheese that I can hardly think. If we hadn't invited Marcus to eat with us, we'd be home by now. I wouldn't have this suffocating smell in my nose. I'd be enjoying a hot shower. That's all I'm thinking about. Taking a shower.

CHAPTER 3

The thing of it is, you're not there when it happens. Not conscious of it, anyway. Which makes it doubly hard to believe.

All I know is, I'm dead tired when I get out of the shower. I guess this is what the flu does to you. Also, I can smell the cheese again. I've scrubbed and rinsed and it makes no difference. I'm too tired to think about it anymore, so I hit the bed. When I wake up, the odor is gone.

But I'm not in bed. I'm on the floor. It's still night. The lamp is on. Dad and Chopper are both looking down at me, their faces white and serious. Chopper is wearing his dorky pajamas but he still has his glasses on.

"Do you know who I am?" Dad asks.

Is this a joke? "You're Marcus, right? No, wait—Wrong color. You must be—"

Dad is not amused. "Who am I? I'm serious."

"What is this, the Inquisition?"

"Are you all right?" Chopper asks.

"I'm fine." I sit up and look around. "What am I doing on the floor?"

"You don't remember?"

"Remember what?"

I rub my mouth because my lip feels wet, and my hand comes away bloody. I notice then that my tongue hurts like hell.

"You bit your tongue," Chopper says.

"Duh."

"You threw yourself out of bed and started shaking," he says. "We heard you hit the floor."

"What time is it?" The digital red numbers on my clock are faced away from me. Dad turns the clock so I can see. Eleven thirty-two. I went to bed half an hour ago.

"Your eyes were rolled back and your ears were blue and you were shaking," Chopper continues. "I thought you were dying." He takes off his glasses and cleans them on the corner of his pajama top, studying me all the time like I'm some kind of interesting bug.

"Then you opened your eyes and stood up. You walked around the room thrashing your arms." He puts his glasses on and flails his arms to demonstrate. "Then you lay back down on the floor and acted like you were sleeping except you were breathing funny. Snorting." He snorts a couple of times. "Then you woke up."

"Very funny, Chopper."

"He's not joking," Dad says.

"Jesus," I say. "How long did this go on?"

"It felt like forever," Dad says.

"Less than ten minutes," Chopper informs me. "Probably more like five. We were about to call 911 but then you started walking around and by the time we realized you were completely spazzed out, it was over."

Dad sits on my bed and gives me an earnest look. "Tell me the truth, Jake. What's going on? Have you been taking drugs? You might as well tell me, because if you are, I'm going to find out."

During wrestling season? Is he kidding? I'm wide awake now, getting mad.

17

"Hell, yes, I've been taking drugs. I took that antibiotic so I wouldn't get some infection to go along with the flu. I took that cough medicine. I took about a ton of Tylenol and decongestant and antihistamine and— "

"That's it, then," Dad says. "That explains it."

"I haven't taken any of it since last week."

"You could have had a delayed reaction. I've read that drug reactions are sometimes delayed." Dad doesn't know diddley about drug reactions and his face is so pale that I see he's in serious denial mode. This is getting scary.

"Also, he hit his head," Chopper says.

Dad turns toward him and stares blankly. I point to my ear. "When I was wrestling."

"Does it hurt?" Chopper asks.

"I've hit it harder than this before. How do you think my ear got to look like this?" I run a finger along the misshapen cartilage. "Anyway, I had my headgear on."

At the moment, what hurts is not my ear but my tongue. I get up and check it out in the mirror. There's a jagged cut on the right side, nothing much for as bad as it feels. My mouth tastes like blood.

"Well, maybe a reaction to the medicines combined with hitting his head," Dad says.

"I think we should call Dr. Crystal," Chopper offers.

I look at him, away from the mirror. "Why?" Aside from the tongue, I feel fine.

"I think we should at least see what she says."

"I think we should go back to bed," I say.

Which, in the end, is what we do.

• • •

In the morning Dad is cooking bacon. The smell

fills the house, but it's a nice smell, normal. Not like the cheese.

"You okay?" he asks.

"Yeah, fine. You didn't go to work?" He's in sweatpants and a sweatshirt, needs a shave.

"I was off last night, remember? I called Dr. Crystal earlier, but she's out of town."

"Earlier? It's seven fifteen. It *is* earlier."

Dad lifts the frying pan off the stove and pours the grease into a can. "I got the answering service. Dr. Petker called me back."

Weighty silence except for the sizzling of bacon grease. Dr. Petker is the junior partner, the one Dad termed an incompetent piece of flab after he told Mom she had a broken rib and it turned out to be pneumonia.

"So?"

"He thinks it was night terrors. Usually kids have them, but it can happen when you're older."

"Night terrors?"

"It's when you wake up and scream or run around like you're trying to escape from a nightmare, or else terrified of what's in the room. But you're not conscious. He says it can happen sometimes after a sickness. Maybe a reaction to all those medicines and bumping your head. Just like we thought."

"Yeah. Well, good."

"How would it explain his spazzing out on the floor, then?" Chopper is standing in the kitchen doorway, frowning.

"Spazzing out?" I ask.

"He says if it were anything but night terrors Jake wouldn't have walked around like that, and would have felt

19

worse when he woke up. Been disoriented and exhausted, and maybe had an upset stomach."

"How do we know he doesn't have a concussion?" Chopper stuffs the bottom of a wrinkled Marine Corps T-shirt into too-loose jeans.

"I'd feel worse," I say. "I had that concussion in fifth grade when I fell off the monkey bars. I was dizzy for two days. Wicked headache. Now I'm fine except for my mouth."

Chopper looks at Dad. "When does Dr. Crystal come back?"

"Next week." Dad lifts pieces of bacon out of the pan, onto a paper towel to drain. "Dr. Petker said he knows it's scary but it's probably nothing. You want your eggs over easy or scrambled?"

"Scrambled," Chopper replies.

"Sit down, then. Don't make a mountain out of a molehill. Dr. Petker said we could come in and go through a bunch of tests and probably come up with nothing. Or we can assume it's some one-time freak reaction to being sick for two weeks and thumping his head. He says he's seen this before."

Chopper grumbles, but he sits. Dad scrambles a bunch of eggs and makes toast for us. When the eggs are ready, Chopper eats like he's starving. When Dad finally sits down to his own breakfast, Chopper says, "Just remember. You're taking advice from a doctor fifty pounds overweight who tells people how to diet."

• • •

Later, when I come home from practice, Chopper is in his room at the computer. Even though the house is freezing, he's still in the short-sleeved shirt he put on this morning. It's from the Marine Corps mountain warfare school where one of Dad's friends went, a washed-out shirt with a drawing of a skeleton whose physique resembles Chopper's, and the single word: *Survival*. A pile of print-outs sits on Chopper's desk, and the computer screen glows blue with what looks like a database. While his friends play games and find dirty pictures to use as screen savers, Chopper surfs the Net, explores libraries, spends hours upgrading his home page. A Faith Hill song blares from his CD-ROM drive. He spots me and turns down the volume.

"It wasn't night terrors," he says. "It was a seizure."

"A seizure!"

He flips the CD out of the drive. "You bit your tongue. It's the classic tell-tale sign. People who have night terrors don't bite their tongue."

I'm not believing this. "Do people who have seizures get up and walk around in the middle of them?"

"Not usually, but it can happen. The brain can make you do all kinds of things." He types a few keystrokes and then turns back to me. "Did you have any other symptoms?"

"Like what?"

"Did you feel weird?"

"I didn't even know it happened until it was over," I say.

"I mean before."

"Not particularly."

"Tired? In a strange mood?"

"Nothing earth-shaking." Then I remember. "Except for the cheese."

"The cheese?" Chopper stares at me blankly.

21

"The pizza cheese. It smelled gross. The smell kept coming and going even in the car and after I took a shower."

"Maybe it was an aura, then, or that other thing, that— "

"Say what?"

"Some people, before they have a seizure, they smell something bad or they feel wildly happy or they see dots in front of their eyes. That's how they know what's coming. Then they have the seizure and afterwards the feeling is gone."

A chill works its way from the base of my neck down my spine.

"With seizures you can lose bladder or bowel control, too."

"You're telling me I was lucky I didn't take a crap in my pants?"

"Yeah, you were."

"That's real comforting."

"Well, check this out. Ten percent of the population has a single seizure at some time in their life and it never happens again."

"Yeah?" The little shiver of fear calms down.

"So even if Dr. Petker was wrong about his diagnosis, he was right that it's nothing to go running for tests about."

"Worrywart," I tell him.

"Jock."

"Dork-nose."

We grin. Like Dad said, no point making a mountain out of a molehill. Chopper's three years younger than me, and even though he's a computer whiz who can get hold of tons of information on any given subject, who's to say he understands it? Even if he does, the worst thing he's telling me is that something happened last night that probably won't ever happen again. No problem.

Dad, who's been taking a nap, appears in the door-way, wearing the same sweats he had on this morning. "Why the merriment?"

Chopper tells him, and Dad nods. "We probably don't need to mention this to Mom, then," he says.

We wouldn't have anyway. Not telling Mom goes without saying.

CHAPTER 4

The next day is Honor Society induction. We find this out when we get to school and Mr. Bodie, the principal, announces an assembly for the senior class. Right away everyone knows what's going on. The guidance counselors have called the parents of the chosen few and invited them to the ceremony. The parents have arrived early and gathered in the cafeteria so their kids won't see them and know they're about to be tapped. As far as I'm concerned, it's just more bad news after my night terrors or seizure or whatever it was. I didn't get into Honor Society last spring and won't be getting in now since I didn't reapply.

But for my girlfriend, Callie, who also missed out last time, this could be a red-letter day. Or not. When she catches up with me in the hall on the way to the auditorium, the hand she slips into mine is cold and covered with sweat, and her face is even paler than usual.

"You're in," I whisper.

"I hope so." Her voice sounds like it's about to crack.

"The Mackerel's not going to keep you out again," I tell her. "She doesn't have it in for anyone who's finished with her class. I bet you anything."

"Anything?" Callie tries to cheer up. "Your car for a year? A trip to the Bahamas?"

"Maybe not *anything*." I squeeze her hand. If things

don't go well for her, maybe later I'll confess to her about my late-night shakies, take her mind off her troubles.

But—wait a minute. What am I thinking? The Chapman family has one strict rule: never tell personal secrets. You never know when they'll come back to haunt you. As a teenager, Dad once lost a summer job because he blabbed that he'd wrecked his car the year before. The job wasn't supposed to involve driving, but the bosses decided it would, and he was out. "A word to the wise," he always says.

"Wish me luck," Callie whispers.

I do, and let go of her hand so she can sit with her homeroom. As she walks away, she tosses her head as if she doesn't have a care in the world. Her hair flops down against her shoulders, black and bouncy and hopeful-looking.

I find a seat just as Mr. Bodie walks to the podium. In his best principal-voice he begins his speech about excellence, scholarship, leadership. I'm about to zone out when a spike of anger zips through me: Me, Jake Chapman, seventh in the senior class, who only has to pass his physical to be an official recipient of a Navy ROTC scholarship worth sixty thousand dollars, the amazing scholar/athlete on his way to being Maynard High's most valuable wrestler – could this be the same guy who wasn't worthy of being admitted into National Honor Society last spring?

But I am. And the reason I didn't get in was no secret to anyone. A Mackerel Attack. One of the worst.

"I wish you wouldn't call her The Mackerel," Mom always used to tell me. "You might not like her, but a teacher is still entitled to be called Ms. Macris."

"To her face, maybe," I said.

E. M. J. Benjamin

The Mackerel taught Advanced Placement English. She hated me from the beginning. Before the first month was over, I was on her famous List. To stay off it you had to suck up to her big-time. Come to her for special help with every theme. Pretend to enjoy her talking politics instead of English. Fake admiration for her old-time capital-letter Feminism no matter how much it offended you personally, as on the days she gushed with pleasure every time some girl was mentioned on the announcements but ignored any boy who was singled out, especially if he happened to be (ugh) a jock.

When I was named Outstanding Wrestler at the Midwinter Invitational and Mr. Bodie told the whole school about it over the loudspeaker, The Mackerel never said a word. Considering how many of my classmates said "good job, Jake" or something to that effect, it was all she could do to pretend it hadn't happened. But when the girls' basketball team won a tournament a week later, she fell all over herself congratulating the three team members in our class. The Mackerel gave me decent grades because I earned them. But it must have nearly killed her, given her inability to speak to me without a heavy dose of sarcasm.

"Ah, the jock comes to class today," she said after I'd been away two days for regionals. "No excused absence for another meet today? Well! What good fortune!"

Before long I was accorded her harshest treatment, one you'd think belonged only in elementary school – the pig face. This was a stand-up paper pig with a three-dimensional pink snout that we'd find on our desks any time she decided our work was "sloppy" – which could mean anything from sloppy handwriting on a quiz to "sloppy thinking" on a paper. You'd think someone would have complained, but the humiliation was such that it wasn't something you wanted to own up to in the principal's office. And it was reserved exclusively for The List – me, Paul Johannsen who played center on the football team, and a few others who'd committed various crimes of political incorrectness or failure to kiss butt.

All the same, I didn't expect her to keep me out of Honor Society. My class rank was too high; I had too much going for me. Or so I thought. At the end of the tapping ceremony when I realized I really wasn't going to get in, I was honestly stunned. But I handled it pretty well. Made a few jokes to Tom Bennett sitting beside me. Told myself it was one of Life's Little Tests. Got up with the others when the assembly was over, ready to face the world.

Callie wasn't so stoic. As we filed out of the auditorium – the inductees to the cafeteria where they'd have cookies and punch with their proud families, the rest of us back to our classes – I noticed she was still in her seat. She was a loner in English class, never laughed at The Mackerel's jokes, probably didn't ask for help on her themes, either. I didn't know Callie well, but I'd always thought she was pretty together. I figured it took some powerful emotion to keep her riveted to her seat even after the assembly was over. Without thinking, I started in her direction.

It wasn't until I got close that I noticed tears streaming down her face. The way she sat there, you'd think she wasn't aware of them herself. She wasn't sobbing or making any noise. She wasn't trying to wipe the tears away. She was just staring up at the stage where the new Honor Society members had gotten their certificates a few moments ago, before they went downstairs to celebrate with their parents.

"Hey, welcome to the Outsiders Club," I said. "To the Band of the Unworthy."

She tried to smile, but her mouth wasn't in it.

"Did you ever hear the commercial about the sad little flounder who isn't good enough to be served at Brownie's Restaurant?" I asked. "Where the big honcho fish-buyer rejects him?"

This was weak, but it was the best I could do under the circumstances. Callie looked at me quizzically.

"That's us, isn't it? Except in this case we're talking about Mackerel and not flounder."

She nodded, but the tears kept coming.

"What those sad little fish didn't know," I went on, "is that all they were missing was being grilled with the other 'superior' flounder, so people like us could have them for dinner."

"I sure hope so," she whispered. She didn't move, didn't smile. I sat down next to her.

One thing I discovered right then was, you don't know what the girl of your dreams is going to look like until you meet her. I've always liked brown-eyed blondes with tawny skin. Callie's hair is black, her eyes are green, and her skin is so white that until you get used to it, she looks like she's sick or about to faint – except when she cries, in which case her face becomes a red splotch, as it was then.

"Don't look at me," she said when she noticed me staring. "I look horrible."

"In the Band of the Unworthy, you don't have to be ugly, but it helps."

She sniffed, got control of her voice. "My sister dropped out of school at sixteen. She still hasn't gotten her

GED. I was counting on this to show her somebody in the family could do it."

"Yeah. I was counting on it, too."

She fumbled around in her purse and found a clean tissue. She blew her nose. We sat there a while, not trying to be cheerful.

"I'm number seven in the graduating class," I said. "I thought I had this nailed."

"I'm number nine," she told me. "How many people you think got in? Thirty?"

We stayed in the auditorium until the bell rang and Callie's face stopped being splotchy. While the new Honor Society members ate snacks and accepted congratulations, Callie and I figured out that none of the eight people on The Mackerel's List got tapped. None. We talked about possible avenues of revenge. We decided against them. The best revenge was not letting The Mackerel know we cared.

I didn't know then that Callie's sister had dropped out of school because she was pregnant, or that now she has a five-year-old son and a job at Bailey's Drugs. I didn't know Callie was expected to do all the things Peggy hadn't. All I knew was that seeing her cry and being able to joke her out of it took the sting out of that day.

We've been together ever since.

The next day in English, it became obvious that some of the parents had called to complain about their sons or daughters not making Honor Society. The Mackerel spent most of the period defending herself. She told us that a lone faculty member could not keep a student out of Honor Society. It had to be done by a majority vote. "A single teacher is just a small, single voice," she protested.

We were not impressed. We'd seen her manipulate

people. "Don't be afraid to ask for help on your themes," she'd cajole in class, in a sweet voice that gave no hint of how vengeful she'd be if you decided you could write your papers yourself. We figured she had the Honor Society committee under her thumb. That day, she tried to sound sincere, even apologetic. "Honestly, class, there was nothing I could do." The kids who'd gotten into Honor Society believed her. Those on her List didn't. She didn't seem to care. Directing her gaze first to one of us and then another, she fixed us with an expression that said, very clearly: *Gotcha!*

Later, Dad said to me, "Sometimes things happen that you can never make up for, Jake. You can't retaliate. You're just . . . caught. You wait them out. You try to learn from them. That's all you can do."

And I guess I did learn. When it came time to fill out the form to be reconsidered for Honor Society this fall, I decided to pass. By then I'd been offered my scholarship. I'd gotten early acceptance to State, which is the only place I wanted to go. I'd done better on the AP exam than most of The Mackerel's favorites, which I know galled her. She had no power over me anymore, and I sure wasn't going to give her any.

But to Callie, all that mattered was proving to her sister and her mom that their family was good enough, that she could do it.

Now, as we sit waiting for the fall inductees to be tapped, I try to catch a glimpse of Callie across the auditorium, send her good vibes. But all I can see is a hank of black hair.

On stage, the current Honor Society members are dressed in borrowed graduation gowns to make them look scholarly. At a signal from one of the teachers, they move down into the audience so they can tap the new inductees as their names are called.

The person who comes to the microphone to read the list is The Mackerel.

She's dressed in a wine-colored suit instead of her usual long hippie-skirt, and she lowers her voice as if she's been taking drama lessons. You can tell she's in her glory. "Alissa Barnes," she intones.

The Honor Society member assigned to Alissa taps her shoulder. Alissa gets up. Together the two of them move down the aisle towards the stage while The Mackerel reads a list of Alissa's accomplishments. Alissa goes up the steps and lights the candle someone gives her. The Mackerel turns back to her list.

"George Parham," she says.

Another gownie moves toward George. They go through the same routine, the same candle-lighting. Then two more names. Three.

The ceremony feels like it's going to take forever.

So when someone finally stops at Callie's row and The Mackerel calls, "Calpurnia Harris," I realize I've been holding my breath.

Callie inches out of her seat. She holds her head high and moves into the aisle. The Mackerel's voice sounds strangled as she tells about Callie's grade point average and her participation in the Maynard Singers. She sounds as if she's about to smother.

I love it.

When the ceremony is over, Callie's mother appears from the back of the auditorium and rushes toward the stage. Mother and daughter embrace. There's a lot of parental embracing. I go up to congratulate Callie, too.

"I knew you'd make it," I tell her. "The Mackerel forgot she hated you until she had to say your name."

"She must have a new bunch to pick on," Callie says. For once, her face is full of color.

A minute later Callie and Mrs. Harris are swept into the line of people making their way toward the reception. One of the guidance counselors holds her arm out to separate me from them, to bar my way. "You're supposed to go back to class," she says.

"It's okay, he's my boyfriend," Callie says. "He's—"

"Parents and Honor Society only," the counselor insists.

Callie looks forlorn. I shrug and wave her on. I move away.

What a joke.

CHAPTER 5

As if Honor Society and a case of the shakies weren't misery enough, I can't even enjoy wrestling practice. Coach Lindy is late, so we spend an eternity doing conditioning exercises with his assistant, Coach Wallace, one of the million JV football coaches who know zip about wrestling.

Finally Coach Lindy shows up and goes right into takedown drills, another thing we do forever and ever. "Think what a takedown is and you'll see why it's so important," he growls when someone complains. "It's that critical moment when you get the other guy off balance and take him to the mat. The critical moment when you get control and your opponent has to go on the defensive."

We hear these words at least a dozen times a day.

Coach circles the mat like some predatory animal. "The move is worth only two points, so why get excited?" He jabs his index finger in our direction. "Because more often than not, the guy who gets the first takedown will win the match. Because he makes his opponent lose confidence and wonder if he can ever regain control." He stabs the air one more time. "You do enough takedown drills and when you get into an actual match it will be second nature, even with your adrenaline pumping."

Usually, he's right.

That day and for the rest of the week my ear stays

sore from the night I hit it. I'm favoring my right side without realizing it until Coach yells, "For godsake, Jake, put on some headgear." I do, and from that moment on, all my moves feel smoother. The whole team's into a nice working rhythm. I'm actually having a good time.

Then Wanda Caster saunters in, and the good vibes go out of the wrestling room like air out of a balloon.

If Wanda were a guy, Coach Lindy wouldn't just stand there with his cue-ball head sweat-shiny and his bushy red eyebrows raised in mock astonishment. If she were a guy, he'd beckon her close until his big barrel chest was at the level of her eyes, and then he'd offer a few choice words about people who show up halfway through practice and what he thinks of them. It wouldn't be pretty.

But he doesn't say a word. He ignores her even after she gets onto the mats. She's the first girl who's ever come out for wrestling, and the rules say we have to take her. You'd think anyone with common sense would watch a few wrestling holds and think about the objective – getting an opponent flat on his back while lying on top of him – and decide this is not a game boys and girls should play together. But there is such a thing as Gender Equity. Coach won't say this outright, but the general feeling is that Wanda Caster is a lawsuit waiting to happen.

Fortunately, she doesn't show up every day. She did at first, but then she started coming three, four days a week, sometimes less. Coach could cut her for this if he wanted, but he won't, and not just because she could sue for discrimination. Coach doesn't cut anybody. He believes people drop out by themselves, once they've decided they aren't tough enough or can't figure it out. But not Wanda. Like The Mackerel, Wanda is a warrior. A hundred-pound warrior shaped like a piece of plywood, straight up and down, a carpenter's dream, with about as much strength as a piece of straw. But a warrior all the same. On the days she decides to grace us with her presence, she hauls her flat, skinny, unmuscular body onto the mat and pretends she's a wrestler like the rest of us.

"Polson, work with Wanda for a while," Coach calls to our freshman lightweight.

"Yeah, Pole," Marcus says. "Go down on Wanda for a while."

Coach shoots him a warning look. Marcus shuts up. Pole blanches. Wanda gets in the down position, on hands and knees, and Pole takes what seems like half an hour adjusting himself behind her, inching one hand around her middle and delicately grasping her elbow with the other, terrified he's going to touch something he shouldn't.

Rumor has it that Wanda told some of her friends the guys at practice are trying to "feel her." This might be true of Brian Fensel, who outweighs her by 60 pounds and leeringly offers to show her a few moves. But most of us are just embarrassed. The whistle blows to begin the drill, and Pole does everything but roll over on his back to avoid touching her. After a few minutes, Coach lets him off the hook and sics Wanda on somebody else.

At the end of practice, Coach calls Pole over to show him something, probably by way of apologizing for making him work out with a girl. Usually freshmen don't get much personal advice.

"Listen, you're new at this, nobody expects you to win," Coach tells him. "But you know enough now that you don't have to get pinned in the first period. Not every time, anyway. You think you're finished long before you are.

You have to stick with it as long as you can."

"I thought I *was* sticking with it."

"Jake, hold him there." Coach motions me to hold Pole in a pinning position on the mat, which is no great feat considering Pole's size and inexperience.

"Now try to get out," Coach says.

Of course Pole can't. Coach lets him struggle until I begin to feel sorry for him.

"Exactly. Now you're out of steam, you're dying out there, you can't move a muscle. Right?"

Pole grunts.

"Good. Now imagine somebody threw a snake over there." He points to the edge of the mat.

I turn my head to him. "Not the snake again."

Coach ignores me and keeps pointing toward the imaginary reptile. "A big one. Man-eating." He opens his arms to indicate the size. "He's licking his chops, see? A freshman, he's thinking. Freshman is his favorite meal."

Coach taps me on the head. "Concentrate on what you're doing."

He gazes down at Pole. "Jake doesn't see the snake because he's trying to pin you. But you— you know it's life or death." He squats down, surprisingly graceful for a man pushing forty. "Now think, Pole. What would you do?"

Pole's face is red, and I think I've pressed the wind out of him. He mutters something unintelligible.

"Exactly!" Coach exclaims with delight. "You'd break that hold and run like hell." He flattens his palm and zooms it in the direction of the exit. "You'd have all the energy in the world. Bet you anything. You're never as tired as you think you are." To me he says, "Okay. Let him go."

Pole gets up, oxygen-deprived and confused.

"That's what you have to think about when you're lying there and the ref is counting back points. Think of the snake coming toward you."

Pole looks at his feet, which he always does when he's insecure. "Yeah, okay. Sure."

"Don't study your feet while I'm talking to you," Coach says. "Study the snake. Give those feet any more attention and they might start growing again." Although Pole weighs only a hundred pounds, his feet are already a size thirteen. If he grows into them, he'll be wrestling heavyweight by the time he's a senior.

Coach cuffs Pole on the shoulder. "The snake," he says again, and walks away.

In the locker room, Pole slumps onto a bench and shakes his head. "He's talking about the other night, isn't he? Man, I was trying to get away from him."

"If he didn't think you could do it, he wouldn't talk to you at all." I shed my workout clothes and put them in my gym bag. The place smells disgusting. The locker room is the armpit of Maynard High, just as Maynard High is the armpit of the three high schools in town. It's so old, even the janitors can't keep it clean.

"When Coach doesn't tell the snake story, he tells the Muhammad Ali story," I say.

"What?"

"When Muhammad Ali was a kid, he saved up money and bought himself a bike. It took a long time, but finally he got it. A new, shiny red bike. A dream come true.

"Not two weeks later he goes out one day and the bike's gone. Somebody stole it. He spent all summer looking for it. He went everywhere, all over his neighborhood, but he never found it. Later, when he started boxing, every guy he was in the ring with, he told himself, that's the kid who stole my bike. It made him mad."

"Yeah, well that might work for some people, but I guarantee you the other night it wouldn't have worked for me. I was dead. Really. I mean, maybe thinking about the bike or the snake would have helped me twitch my toe or something."

"It'll come. I was a sophomore before I started feeling like I was out there for more than a cameo appearance." I sniff the air. Bad as the locker room usually smells, it stinks even worse today.

In fact, the stench is overpowering.

Uh-oh, I think, remembering the cheese.

Don't be paranoid, one part of me says. It always smells like this.

Not so fast, buddy, another part whispers. Just because you're paranoid doesn't mean someone isn't after you.

Then the toilet flushes in one of the stalls right behind us, and a moment later, Brian Fensel emerges. He's dressed in his usual denim jacket with studs, spike bracelets, heavy black boots. He's still hiking up his jeans.

"Jesus, Brian. You ought to warn people before you go in there and take a two-hour crap," I say.

But the truth is, I'm mighty glad to see the source of the odor.

CHAPTER 6

When I get home from practice, Dad's at work and Mom's back from her weekly travels. She's standing in the kitchen, pouring little white cartons of take-out Chinese food into microwaveable bowls. Her shoes are under the table and her purple suit jacket is slung over a chair, but except for the full-length apron she's put on, she's still in her executive's outfit: silk blouse, wool skirt, pearls, earrings. Used to be, she'd shed her good clothes the minute she walked in the house and hang them up so they'd stay fresh. She'd put on jeans and cook up a storm even after working all day at the bank. She'd lecture about the virtues of home cooking and fresh vegetables.

"Jake! The oldest son!" she exclaims, and gives me a peck on the cheek. Chopper says this isn't like her, this bright rah-rah stuff. But I think it just takes her a while to get used to us again, after being away all week.

"Hey, Mom."

She gives me the once-over. "Looks like my absence hasn't done you any harm."

"You say that every week."

She smiles. "See?" Her voice is light and airy. Sometimes, since she got her promotion, I think she sounds younger.

If I had to use one word to describe my mother, it would be *calm*. Nothing throws her. Never did. When

Chopper decided to quit fifth grade and Dad went ballistic, Mom was the one who decided he might start doing his lessons again if he could work on a computer. When Grandpa got Alzheimer's and wandered away from the nursing home, Mom was the one who coaxed him back from the middle of the highway and convinced him his room wasn't so bad. Even the Big Career Move hasn't fazed her, except for this adjustment of getting home at the end of the week.

But lately, I think part of the reason she stays so calm and collected, part of the reason nothing throws her, is because nobody tells her anything that might.

We don't plan this or talk about it. We're just careful. When Mom turns back to the cartons of food, I notice she's got the table set with nice dishes, as if to prove takeout Chinese is no different from home-fried steak or roast beef. I automatically put my mind into caution mode.

"How was practice?"

"Fine. Good." Before she started traveling, she never asked how was practice. Even if I told her, what would it mean to her? Diddley-squat.

She puts the bowls into the microwave, sets the timer, pushes start.

"Chopper, soup's on!" she yells. And then, "I heard you won the other night. Undefeated so far."

"So far." I wonder what she'd think if she knew what else happened the other night. "Aren't you going to give me time to take a shower?" I ask.

"Oh, I forgot." She turns off the microwave. "We can wait. Of course."

After that, things get smoother. We eat with chopsticks, talk about our week, read the messages in our fortune cookies. Then we clean the kitchen. From the time I can remember, Chopper and I always had "jobs." Clear table, wipe counters, sweep floor. Afterwards, Mom would run her hand over the Formica top of the kitchen table, to make sure she couldn't feel any bits of food sticking to it, stuff she called "spragues." It's a matter of pride that no surface in our kitchen is ever polluted with spragues. We've cleaned the kitchen so many times in just this way that I forget we haven't been together since last Sunday.

But Chopper hasn't forgotten. "So how much longer traveling?" he asks Mom as he loads the dishwasher.

"At least until after New Year's. But I'll be here part of December. They don't do training close to the holidays." Mom travels to give seminars to bank trainees, and also to substitute for managers out on leave. Before the Big Career Move, she managed one of the local branches, so she knows what she's doing.

"Yeah. New Year's," Chopper grumbles. "And then what?"

"As soon as the new headquarters is finished, they'll bring people here for training and I'll only have to travel to fill in. You know that."

"Right." Chopper sounds doubtful.

For me, Mom's absence means more chores, but it also gives me more freedom. When Dad's not home, I can do whatever I want, go wherever I please, not have to explain. But Chopper hates things being different. Mom rolls up the sleeves of her blouse a couple more cuff-widths, then plunges her arms into the water and makes her voice cheerful.

"You know, I don't think my being away has hurt anybody. Before, I don't think anyone but me knew that the kitchen floor doesn't clean itself or that food doesn't walk from the store into the refrigerator." She turns and winks at us. "Really, you two. Admit it."

Silence.

"Would you ever have learned to throw in a load of laundry if I hadn't taken this job? Would you ever have cooked a meal?"

"I thought you liked to cook," Chopper says.

"I do. But not when I'm tired. I always worked full-time, but I did most of the housework, too. Look how much you've learned."

We don't tell her about the subs and pizzas we order four times a week or our heart-attack cleanup sessions the night before she comes home. We don't tell her Callie and her friends do the kitchen and bathrooms in exchange for Chopper's online research for their term papers. I dry a pot and make a face at Chopper, but he has no sense of humor about this. Pushing his wire-rimmed glasses up on his nonexistent nose, he looks exactly like a worried owl.

"From my point of view, this experience has been an improvement all around," Mom says as she sloshes another pot through the water.

"Are you saying you took your job to teach us a lesson?" Chopper asks.

"No. I did it for financial reasons. You know that." She made the Big Career Move after Dad's company started downsizing. It was good luck, she told us, that she was offered a promotion just when it seemed Dad's job would disappear. (It didn't, of course.) Someone had to earn tuition for two boys soon to be in college. (Why? Chopper's in the ninth grade and I have a scholorship.) Not many people were offered such a good opportunity at exactly the right time. She said all this in a voice cheerful as wind chimes. She knew we'd all pitch in.

Chopper pours detergent into the dishwasher and looks glum. "Financial," he grumbles. "Everything's financial."

I swat him with my dish towel, make him jump away. "Your *butt* isn't financial," I say.

"Oh yeah?" Chopper grabs another towel and swats me back. "I could sell pictures of any part of my anatomy for millions of dollars. *Especially* my butt. Don't think substantial sums haven't been offered."

"Yeah, it's the big red birthmark that attracts everybody so."

"It would be on every home page on the Web if it weren't for my strong sense of privacy."

"Son," Mom says to Chopper, "I think you overestimate your value on the free market." Which goes to show that, although she's calm, she's not ice. She turns off the water, and the whole front of her outfit is soaked, in spite of the apron.

"If I did dishes in dress clothes, I'd get a half-hour lecture," I tell her.

"I would have changed except the suit had to be cleaned anyway." She heads upstairs to put on something dry.

Chopper snorts. "If everything's financial, why isn't she worried about the cleaning bills? She's not doing it for the money. She loves that job!"

"Better than hating it." There's no discussing this with him. He doesn't like Mom traveling. Doesn't understand it. Wants her to stop. Period. Best to hold my tongue, make my escape. I check the clock. The YMCA's still open. I might as well go lift weights.

One major positive fallout from Mom's Big Career Move is that it's left me in charge of her car, an old Civic that still runs like new. Now that the bank gives Mom a company vehicle, the Civic is practically mine. I take Chopper anywhere he needs to go (which is practically nowhere), and otherwise have the car at my disposal. I grab the keys and head out.

In the weight room, my disposition improves as soon as I start sweating. I like pumping iron, I don't deny it. After three years working at it seriously, lifting weights always makes me feel like I've accomplished something. During wrestling season I don't have much time for it, what with practices and matches, and it's always frustrating that by the end of the season I can never bench as much as I did at the beginning. So I'm glad to be here. This year I've promised myself I'm going to keep up my strength.

I do my workout carefully. Don't let myself kip on the pull-ups. Add an extra set of lat-pulls. Feel pleasantly virtuous and relaxed by the time I get home.

But the first thing I see is Chopper, glowering at the TV instead of working at his computer. He turns to me with a scowl. "If everything is really financial, why don't we treat her job like a business arrangement? Why do we all lie to her? Even Dad."

"So she won't have to worry when she gets here. Because being home is the only time she has to rest."

"It's like we're in a conspiracy," Chopper says.

"Don't be stupid, Chopper."

But he has a point. Dad talked to Mom on the phone three or four times this week, and although he told her about my wrestling win and about going out to supper with Marcus, he never said a word about my rocky night after we got home. And Chopper and I won't mention it, either.

Which is probably okay, since the episode was a one-time thing.

But not telling her stuff is getting to be a habit.

So what does that mean?

CHAPTER 7

Saturday night Callie and I spend the evening at my friend Steven Wills' house, where we watch one of the old Freddy Krueger *Nightmare on Elm Street* movies. Callie hates horror movies and loves them, too. She cuddles close to me on Steven's couch. She screams at the scary parts, and Steven's girlfriend screams, too. When the movie's over, Steven wants us to go rent another tape, but we have to cut the evening short because Callie has a big choir program at church the next morning. When I get home, Chopper's still upstairs at the computer, with Garth Brooks blaring from the CD drive. Dad and Mom have gone out somewhere.

I call Callie and tell her not to let Freddy give her nightmares. I want to hear her soft, throaty laugh. Then I turn on the TV and fall asleep in the family room. I do this a lot. I never recall going up to bed, but somehow I always manage to get there.

In what feels like about five minutes, Chopper's poking at me to get up. I force an eye open. Bright sun pours into my bedroom window. The clock says 9:33. It's Sunday, so I pull the quilt over my head and wave him away.

"Talk to me for one minute. I know you're hung over, but it won't kill you."

"Hung over?" I peer out from under the quilt.

"You were drunk last night. Don't tell me you weren't."

"Yeah. Wasted. From two Diet Pepsis and a handful of pretzels." I feel bad about the pretzels because the salt makes you hold water, and during wrestling season I'm always watching my weight.

"Diet Pepsi. Right." He sits on the side of my bed and sniffs as if he expects to smell beer.

"Since when do I drink when I'm wrestling? What's wrong with you? Go back to bed."

"Ssshh." He puts his index finger to his lips and points to Mom and Dad's room. "Remember when you fell asleep downstairs?"

"Sort of."

"Do you remember coming up?"

"I never remember. But here I am. Amazing, huh?"

"You were walking like a drunk person. You were slurring your words."

"I was half-asleep."

"No. You were drunk. I asked you what you were doing and you said, 'I dunna,' " – he weaves around the room to demonstrate – "and then you started to get in bed with all your clothes on."

"Right. And I reeked of whiskey." I wonder if he's making this up. Some people will do anything for a joke.

"I asked if you wanted to take your clothes off before you got in bed and you said no. You got under the covers and buried your head in your pillow. When I asked what was wrong, you said you were afraid. I asked you of what and you said of Freddy."

He can't be making this up. Callie's the one who's afraid of Freddy, not me, but Chopper didn't know what movie we were going to watch.

"Then you sort of . . . woke up, I guess. You were all right. You got undressed and went to sleep."

"It was probably nothing. Maybe I was sleepwalking."

"No. It was weird."

"Relax, Chopper. It was nothing. You should hear yourself. Maybe I was sleepwalking and having a bad dream." It's hard to be concerned about something that happens when you aren't there.

I nod my head in the direction of Mom and Dad's room. "Do they know?"

"No. I must have gone to sleep before they came in."

"Good." Without saying anything else, we both know we aren't going to tell them.

• • •

Two days later we have the first of our two matches with Riverside High. Riverside is our cross-town rival. It sits on a big wooded campus with its own stadium and a new track, while Maynard High is in the middle of town, with no campus, a 50-year-old wrestling room, and such rundown practice fields that we have to play soccer and football in the municipal stadium.

Worse, Riverside wins the conference wrestling championship almost every year, despite the antics of their coach, Coach Kimball, better known as Fuzzball. Fuzzball plays more mind-games with other teams than anyone in the conference. He moves his wrestlers to different weights not just to give them a better chance to win, but to be unpredictable. He spreads rumors about other coaches being dishonest. He tells the newspapers his wrestlers have gotten scholarships even when they haven't. The annoying thing is, in spite of his faults he's a dynamite recruiter. His team is always three or four deep in every weight class. And his kids are good.

But this year we think we've got a chance against them. With four seniors and a couple of experienced juniors, we're stronger than we've been for a long time. We've got decent guys at weights where Riverside is weak. Although the conference championships are three months off, we're all anxious to check out Riverside's strength.

The mood on the bus is manic, partly because we're antsy and partly because Wanda Custer hasn't appeared. What luck! It's hard to believe how one girl can make a bus full of wrestlers feel muzzled. For once, nobody even minds when Brian Fensel starts with his stupid "Yo momma" jokes.

He pokes Keith Garcia, who's sitting in front of him.

"Yo momma's so fat she puts on her lipstick with a paint roller," he says.

"Oh, yeah?" Keith grins.

"Yo momma's so fat, when she sits on the beach, Greenpeace shows up and tries to throw her back in the ocean." Brian runs his hand over his greasy hair, slicked back into a duck-tail like something out of the '50s, to go with his denim and studs and motorcycle boots. "Yo momma's so fat that when she stands up she's in two time zones. She's so fat the National Weather Service has to assign names to her farts."

Somebody laughs. Brian points to Pole. "Yo momma's so ugly she looked out the window and got arrested for mooning. She's so old she knew Burger King when he was a prince." He turns his attention to Marcus. "Yo momma's so fat and so stupid her waist is bigger than her IQ. Her head's so big that when she changes her mind, she has to leave the room."

Although most of the guys are laughing now, in the seat beside me Marcus stiffens. He leans forward to jab Brian in the shoulder. "Chill, man." Not that this is logical, but I know Marcus has stopped thinking of Brian's one-liners as jokes and started thinking of them as personal insults. Nobody makes cracks about Marcus' mother. If he thought about it a second, it might occur to him that "Yo Momma" jokes are purely generic. But at times like these, Marcus is not given to cool analysis.

Coach Lindy could calm him down, but he isn't here. His rule is that everyone has to ride the activity bus to cross-town meets, even those of us who have cars. It's good for team spirit. But Coach drives his own station wagon over and lets Coach Wallace drive the bus. That way, Coach Lindy can make some of us ride with him back to school after the meet, whichever ones he thinks need a lecture.

"Yo Momma so ugly she could make an onion cry," Brian says.

"I told you – shut the hell up!" Marcus yanks the longish duck-tail at the back of Brian's head. Brian jerks away.

"Yo momma so ugly that—"

Marcus reaches over the seat and claps a hand over Brian's mouth. He pulls Brian back against the cushion in a kind of headlock. "Keep your mouth shut before I kick your fat ass."

"Mmmph," Brian mutters as he tries to break free. He's bigger than Marcus, but Marcus has him in a stranglehold.

"Keep it shut, man, I mean it."

"Cut it out!" Coach Wallace bellows, glaring at us in the rearview mirror.

Marcus lets Brian go. He sits back and tries to look innocent.

"What's your problem, asswipe?" Brian asks, rubbing his mouth.

"You're my problem, greaseball," Marcus says.

"Dick," Brian mumbles.

"Shut up, fat boy."

"Save it for Riverside," I whisper, low enough so only Marcus can hear. Now that Marcus has gotten started, I don't expect him to stop, but for some reason, he does.

• • •

Riverside has a lot of wrestlers, so we have a whole JV match before the regular meet starts. Even in the JV matches, Coach Fuzzball is in high form. Any time one of his wrestlers is tired, he bounces up and questions the ref's call, just long enough for his guy to get a breather. He's about five foot five and so fat and hairy he truly looks like a walking fuzzball. Curly black chest hairs pop out of the top of his shirt, and his arms and legs are covered with what looks like fur. All in all, he makes a good argument for compulsory body-shaving. His pudgy arms pump wildly as he crosses the gym. He stops practically in the ref's face. Twice he claims our guy has made an illegal move when he hasn't. Anything to get the mental edge. And this in the preliminaries!

Then, in the first regular match of the evening, an amazing thing happens. Pole wins. He's wrestling a sophomore who ought to whomp him, but when he gets turned to his back like he usually does, somehow he fights out of it, reverses the kid, and pins him. We're up six to nothing.

"I was thinking about the snake," Pole gasps when he comes off the mat.

"About time," Coach tells him. And we're on a roll.

We're still ahead when we get to the 140-pounders. Marcus takes his lucky earring out of his ear and puts it in a plastic baggie for safekeeping. The earring is a plain gold stud, something he could get anywhere, but if he lost it he'd be frantic. Then he goes out to the mat looking like he couldn't care less, but he's up against Earl Summers, who's good, and he knows he has his work cut out for him. "Keep the underhook!" Coach keeps yelling when the match gets underway. "Stay basic. Get to your base!"

It's hard to hear with your headgear on, but if you focus on Coach's voice, usually you can. Then the Riverside fans start the obnoxious foot-stomping they do whenever things heat up, and nobody can hear a thing. Coach switches to his famous hand signals. He jumps out of his chair and acts like he's wrenching a guy down; he makes spiraling motions with his arms. Marcus doesn't have a clue what he means and neither do the rest of us. Some of the spectators begin looking at Coach instead of the wrestlers.

I'm trying to watch and warm up at the same time, fighting my usual case of nerves. I'm wearing my good-luck T-shirt, the Marine Corps shirt that says "Bad to the Bone." I know Riverside's 145-pounder is a year behind me and not that good, so I shouldn't be this panicky, but I am. At the end of third period, Marcus is down by one. It doesn't look good. Then he gets a reversal – two points – and wins. Our fans cheer wildly.

Instead of leaving well enough alone, Marcus keeps his hand raised in victory after he leaves the mat and takes a slow saunter past Riverside's stands. He grabs his crotch like Michael Jackson and humps a few times in the direction of Riverside's fans. Then he struts back to our bench.

Coach Lindy can't believe it. A crimson flush rises from the base of his neck up his face and across his entire bald head. He grabs Marcus by his singlet and sends him to the locker room.

Coach Fuzzball goes wild. "Did you see that?" he shouts at the ref. "Did you? Did you?" He points to the locker room, flails his arms like a madman.

In the end, the ref docks our team a point for Marcus's unsportsmanlike conduct. Even though I win by a pin and so does Brian Fensel, at the end of the night that one point costs us the meet.

Coach Lindy won't talk to Marcus at all, even though Marcus keeps trying to apologize. At the end of the meet he motions him to ride back to school in his station wagon instead of the bus. He also beckons to me and Pole. When he's got something to say to one guy, he always figures a couple of others can benefit from hearing it.

He makes Marcus sit in the front and doesn't utter a word for the first five minutes of the ride. It seems like forever. Then he looks in the rearview mirror at me and Pole and says in this deep flat voice that makes chills run up my spine, "You know the best thing about high school sports? It's that it has zero consequences."

He lets us ponder this for a minute. Marcus is starting to squirm.

"Yes sir, high school sports are something you can

really get up for, really get excited about, and when it's all over you've learned something and there's no downside at all."

We stop at a light and he turns around to look at Pole directly. "Your first win. Feels great, doesn't it? You're on top of the world. Right?"

"Yeah, I guess."

"You don't really even care that the team lost, do you?"

"Well, sure I— "

"The whole team could get pinned and as long as you won your own match you'd walk out feeling fine," he says, brushing aside Pole's objections as the light changes and we start off again. "You wouldn't be able to make a big deal out of it on the bus going home, but inside you'd feel great."

The only sound is the whir of traffic traveling along beside us.

"Tell him, Jake. You always feel great when you win. Even if the team bombs."

"You feel okay," I say.

"More than okay." He focuses on Pole again. "You're high. You're happy. You're stoked. Right?"

Pole examines his gigantic feet. "I guess."

"What you're going to find out is, tomorrow nobody's really going to care. And next time you wrestle you're likely to come away feeling as lousy as you feel good tonight. You know what you're going to learn that you can take with you the rest of your life? A sense of perspective."

"Yeah, I guess," Pole agrees.

Marcus is fidgeting seriously now. What he hates most is being ignored.

"You win and you think it's the most important thing in the world," Coach goes on. "You lose and you think it's the end of the world. But in high school sports it's not. The consequences are zero. Zero." He lifts his right hand from the steering wheel and makes an O with his thumb and index finger.

Just when we decide the lecture is over he turns to Marcus. His voice drops a notch. "Idiocy like your stunt tonight doesn't cost much when it's just a wrestling match, Marcus. You're very lucky."

Marcus looks out the window.

"A team point, but hey— You have to keep it in perspective. Right?"

"I'm sorry, Coach," Marcus says. "I said I was sorry."

"I'm sorry too. We had a chance to beat Riverside for the first time in three years. A good chance. Yes, sir. But it doesn't matter, does it? It's over. We wrestle them again before the conference championships. So who cares? We'll have other opportunities."

Marcus begins to take a deep breath but Coach doesn't let up. "Of course for you, next year, it won't be wrestling. It won't even be that stun gun caper with just a slap on the hand. You'll make some dumb gesture and next thing you know you'll lose your job. Or you'll be in a bar and some guy will pull out a .38 and shoot your sorry ass."

Marcus' hand wanders along the controls on the passenger door. He starts to roll down the window. Freezing air rushes in. He rolls it up.

"What I'm saying, Marcus," Coach continues, "is that this is the last time it's going to have zero consequences. If you're going to learn to control yourself in the

55

heat of the moment, you have to learn it now."

"Yeah," Marcus mumbles. Coach puts on his turn signal. We reach the corner and take the right that puts us in sight of Maynard High's parking lot. Marcus sighs with relief.

I don't think much about it at the moment, but later Coach's words will come back to me many times. This is the last time it's going to have zero consequences.

CHAPTER 8

It happens two days later, the day before the next match. Dad's working the night shift, but before he goes he makes spaghetti for supper, which is what I usually eat if I have to wrestle the next day. Spaghetti doesn't put on weight, don't ask me why. He takes some of Mom's sauce out of the freezer and adds his special spices. He's still not much of a cook, so the spices make the house smell rank, but we eat his concoction without complaining. My weight is pretty good, so I don't bother to run before I go to bed. I turn in early, and half-remember Dad saying goodbye.

Next thing I know, the gray light of dawn is coming into the window, and I'm trying to wake up but have trouble opening my eyes. If I didn't feel so bad, I'd think I was dreaming. My stomach feels nasty, and the side of my mouth is on fire – probably from that rotten spaghetti sauce. Then I see Chopper standing over me, peering down with a strange expression on his face. I taste the blood on my tongue and know exactly what's happened.

"You're all right," Chopper says. "At least you didn't throw yourself out of bed this time."

I'm too tired to move. "I think I'm going to puke." I motion him to hand me the trash can.

"This one wasn't as bad. You woke me up hitting your hand against the wall." He knocks against the wall in a rhythmic pattern. "You shook some, but you stayed in one place."

"I feel like crap."

"Yeah, well you sort of look like it, too."

I lean over the trash can, but I don't have the energy to throw up.

"Think of it as a brainstorm," he says. "A storm. It knocks you around."

Even with the nausea, I still feel like I'm dreaming. Like I'm connected to what's going on in the room only by the thinnest thread.

"It lasted just under two minutes. From what I've read, that's about average."

I notice then that Chopper has his watch on. He doesn't sleep with it, so he must have heard me and put it on deliberately, to time it.

I feel like a scientific specimen.

I roll over, look at my clock. Five after seven. Ten minutes before I have to get up.

Next thing I know, it's quarter to eight and Chopper is shaking me awake. He must have turned off my alarm. He's dressed in a red "Semper Fi" T-shirt and jeans; his hair is combed. "I have to go to school now, but you can stay in bed. Sometimes it takes a while to feel normal, afterwards."

"No kidding." My mouth hurts. My stomach is in rebellion. I stumble into the bathroom and vomit into the toilet.

Afterwards, I wash my mouth out at the sink and examine my tongue, which feels like someone's run it through a shredder. Chopper's right behind me, the curious scientist. I'm about to tell him to leave me alone when he hands me a towel and I realize I've forgotten to turn off the spigot. I'm standing in front of the mirror, looking at a face too white to be mine.

"Dad'll be home in a little while," he says. "I could stay until he comes."

"No, I'm all right."

I make my way back to bed. Before Chopper leaves I ask him, "Did that spaghetti sauce bother you last night?"

"No. Why?"

"I mean, didn't the smell of it get to you? While it was cooking?"

"Not especially."

"It smelled gross. It about drove me crazy."

Chopper nods. "Smelled sort of like the other time? The pizza cheese?"

Exactly.

A stab of fear runs through me, but I'm so tired that by the time Chopper's out of the room, I'm almost asleep. I sleep for hours. I'm vaguely aware of Dad coming in, saying hello and asking me how I feel. I don't actually wake all the way up until one-fifteen. The first thing I'm aware of is the crackly feel of a piece of paper under my pillow. A scrawled message in Chopper's handwriting reads, "Didn't tell him. Just said you were sick."

Tentatively, I sit up. I'm okay. No stomach ache. No wobblies. Healthy except for the tongue. I get up and take a shower, which washes away all the nastiness. Then I tiptoe into Dad's room, find him sound asleep, leave him a note: *Woke up, felt better. Went to school.*

It's a home meet tonight. If I'm at school even a couple of periods, I'll be able to wrestle. Won't be considered absent for the day.

When I come home after classes, Dad's still sleeping and Chopper's waiting. "Are you going to tell him?" His face looks as white as mine did in the mirror this morning.

"Eventually," I say. I know how Dad will react. He'll say maybe it was Chopper's imagination. Or maybe I had a stomach virus that made me thrash around in my sleep.

Maybe I did.

Then I get a good look at Chopper's expression. Concerned. Puzzled. But mainly scared. It's the same expression he had on his face when I woke up this morning. He's terrified. Of me. His own brother.

"Sure, we'll tell Dad," I say to him. "But first I think we ought to do something else."

"What?"

"Call Mom."

· · ·

Despite having a major career in so many cities around the state, Mom manages to get home in exactly three hours. Then she's furious because none of us are in the house. We're all at the wrestling match, where she finds us about ten minutes after I chalk up an easy win.

"I told you it wasn't an emergency," I say when she motions me over to the sidelines. "I told you I was all right."

"Nevertheless," she says. Then, in front of everyone, she reaches around my sweaty neck and gives me a hug. "I'm glad you *are* all right."

"Aren't you glad I won?"

She grins. "That, too."

Later we have a Major Family Discussion. Chopper does most of the talking, since he was the one who witnessed all three of what he calls my "episodes." He takes off his glasses, cleans them with the bottom of his T-shirt, and sounds like a medical expert on the witness stand. It gives me the creeps that he knows more about what happened than I do. Dad is angry that we didn't tell him about my sounding drunk and slurring my words. Mom is hurt that we didn't tell her anything at all.

"You're so busy," I say. "We didn't want to worry you."

"The fact that you felt you had to keep it from me worries me more."

We spend the next couple of days in medical mode. I see Dr. Crystal, then a neurologist who sends me for tests. I have an MRI - magnetic images of my brain, sort of like an X-ray. For this I have to lie flat in a claustrophobic high-tech tube that gives me a new appreciation for wide open spaces. The clunking noise it makes every time it takes a photo is my only contact with the outside world except for a mirror, which gives me a view of Mom sitting in the room dutifully smiling and waving. Later a nurse tells me there are also "open" MRIs without the creepy tube, but they don't produce such high-quality images, and you have to go somewhere else to get them. Big comfort.

The MRI reveals that I don't have a brain tumor. Welcome news, but nothing I couldn't have figured out without spending an hour in that miniature space capsule.

I also have an EEG, a graph of my brain waves. The night before, I have to stay up so that I'll be "sleep-deprived" for better results – don't ask me why. I spend the night watching TV while lifting Mom's little dumbbells so I won't accidentally doze off.

The technician who runs the test is a babe. Blonde, with slanted aqua eyes, and not much older than I am. She attaches about twenty sensors to the top of my head, each one with a wire going to the machine that records my brain waves. Having her massage my head as she glues the sensors down is not exactly unpleasant.

For nearly an hour I lie on my cot in the dimly-lit EEG room while she sits outside watching my brain being reduced to squiggles on computer paper. She tells me to breathe slowly. I do. She tells me to breathe fast – not difficult considering what she looks like. She shines a strobe light into the room that blinks faster and faster until I'm dizzy.

She tells me to fall asleep.

"Right," I say. "Did you ever try to fall asleep when someone told you to?"

She laughs.

I squinch my eyes shut. What kind of fool would fall asleep under the watchful eyes of a Miss America who's recording if you snore or your mouth drops open or you drool?

I pretend to sleep. She watches the automatic pen recording the activity of my brain. She's not fooled.

"We do need a sleep reading," she says. "If you don't fall asleep, I can give you a sedative."

Suddenly I'm wide awake. Wrestling practice is in a couple of hours. "No sedatives."

"We'll wait."

Despite my determination not to lose consciousness, about a second later I do fall asleep. When I wake up I wonder what kind of man I am, if fatigue is more powerful than the lure of blonde hair and swimming-pool eyes.

● ● ●

My neurologist, Dr. Symmes, is the opposite of babedom. She's got short, rough gray hair and so many wrinkles that she could easily star in a TV commercial about the perils of spending too much time in the sun. But she's okay. At our conference in her office, she pulls my chair next to her desk and relegates Mom and Dad to a couch across the room. She unfolds the stack of computer paper with my EEG tracings and begins explaining them to me.

"This is when you were hyperventilating." She flips through the pages to another place. "This is when you were watching the strobe light."

I look at the tracings, but they don't mean a thing.

"Often in these cases," she says, "the EEG doesn't show anything at all."

I suppose this means that mine does.

"See these spikes?" She points to a place where the lines make high thin triangles. "This is when you were just falling asleep. That's a critical time." She squints at the paper, and a cobweb of wrinkles etches itself deeper into her face. "These spikes are what we're looking for."

Mom and Dad sit stony-faced on the couch. The office is too hot, and Dad keeps sticking his hand inside the collar of his shirt.

"The spikes indicate abnormal brain activity we often see in people who have seizures – spikes that show up as you're getting drowsy . . . as you're falling asleep."

"But I wasn't having a seizure. I wasn't— "

"I know. I'm talking about abnormal activity in your brain, not something we can necessarily see when we look at you. It's helpful when the EEG shows something, because then we know how to treat."

Dad clears his throat. "So he definitely had a seizure."

"From what you've described, I'd say he had two and maybe three." She turns to me. "Usually the behavior during a seizure is pretty much the same every time. It's a little odd that yours varied so much – the generalized seizure, and then the one when your brother thought you were drunk. But of course it can happen." She focuses on Dad. "About ten percent of us have a single seizure and it never repeats."

We nod. I remember Chopper quoting this same statistic.

"So when Dr. Petker thought it was night terrors—" she continues. "We wouldn't have started treatment on the basis of one episode, anyway."

Dad looks relieved.

"A single seizure is just that," Dr. Symmes says, turning her attention back to me. "Repeated seizures we call epilepsy. In your case, partial epilepsy."

"Epilepsy," I repeat. It isn't the first time I've heard the word; it's only the first time I've heard it used in connection with someone who isn't a weirdo or a freak.

"Yes. Epilepsy because the seizures are repeated. Partial because it arises from part of the brain. In your case, the temporal lobe." She taps my temple.

She begins talking about neurons firing in the brain, how this is normal until too many start firing at once. "—a sort of short-circuit." I hear the words, "generalized seizure . . . same as *grand mal*," and I nod as if I'm following, but my mind is zoning out.

Epilepsy. Disease. Shakies in the bedroom in the middle of the night. Maybe in public in the daytime. What could be more disgusting?

"What happens is, the storm starts in one part of the brain and moves to the whole brain – overloads it, so to speak," Dr. Symmes says. "That's why you shake or go rigid."

"Yes, but what causes it?" Mom asks.

"Any number of things. A brain injury caused by an illness. A drug reaction. A blow to the head— "

"Probably from wrestling," Mom accuses.

Uh-oh. Here goes the rest of my life. Then Dr. Symmes raises her hand.

"I'm sure he hits his head all the time," she tells Mom. "So do boys his age who don't wrestle. If this is something that's important to him, he should keep doing it."

One point for Dr. Symmes.

Dad clears his throat. "What are the chances of its going away?" His voice sounds rusty, as if he hasn't used it for a while. "The chances of him never having any more problems from now on?"

"There are plenty of people who have a handful of seizures and then never have them again. In that case, usually the EEG normalizes, too." She stops for a minute. "But we always recommend treatment any time there are recurrent seizures. In a case like Jake's, we usually medicate to get control. We like people to be seizure-free for at least two years, four is better, before we think about stopping the medication."

None of us speak. From now on, I'm going to take drugs. Me, who doesn't drink, doesn't smoke, hardly ever takes so much as an aspirin except when I have the flu.

We leave with a prescription for pills I have to take three times a day, at breakfast, dinner and bedtime – "more towards the beginning and end of the day since your problem seems to come within an hour of going to sleep or waking up."

Dr. Symmes gives me one final, penetrating "this is serious" look that turns her frown lines into craters between her eyebrows. "The most important thing, Jake, is if you forget a pill, take it as soon as you remember. This isn't something you can stop just like that. When it comes time to go off the medicine, you have to wean off it, pill by pill, over a number of weeks. If you stop all of a sudden, you can actually have rebound seizures."

Great. Probably in the middle of class, with the entire school watching.

"Another thing to remember, Jake. This isn't a disease. It's a disorder."

"A disorder," I mimic.

What the hell difference does it make?

CHAPTER 9

On the way home, Mom and Dad try their best to cheer me up, which only makes it worse.

"You heard what she said about some people having a couple of seizures and then no more trouble," Dad says. "I bet that's all it is. It could be hormones, anything."

Mom shoots him a look, but when she turns to me, she adopts her bounciest tone. "She wouldn't start you on such a low dose of medicine if she didn't think it would be easy to control. Really you're very fortunate."

Fortunate. Right. How does she know? In my hand is a pamphlet listing the medicine's side effects, everything from excess peeing to impotence. Impotence! Dr. Symmes made a big deal of saying it's no problem for teenagers, only for middle-aged men. It would be just my luck to be the exception.

I stare out the window at a cold, thin, spitting kind of rain that exactly matches my mood. This could be the pits. Yet at the same time there's this feeling that it's not really happening. How can you believe in something you have to be told about afterwards . . . something that only shows itself while you're absent? Despite the test results, I don't feel any different than before. Nothing has changed. This so-called disorder wouldn't exist if I didn't take other people's word for it.

When we get home, Chopper already knows. Mom

must have called him from the drugstore where we filled my prescription. He takes off his glasses and squints at me hard. "I heard they gave you the wrong brain. The brain of Abby Normal. I always suspected it."

"Mel Brooks, right? The old Frankenstein movie."

"See? Your fits haven't wiped out your memory after all."

"That's because I have an actual brain and not a computer chip like yours. Abby Normal is better than no brain at all."

"Very searing, Jake." He crouches down and lunges toward me in a bad imitation of a wrestling shot. I grab him around the middle, turn him upside down, hold him there for a while.

This turns out to be the high point of the day. At dinner, everyone watches me take my first pill as if they expect me to break out in welts. They're still peering sidelong half an hour later even though there's been no high drama. The house begins to close in on me. Time to make a quick exit. I'll go see if Steve Wills is home.

Just as I'm about to walk out the door, Mom appears from nowhere. She blocks my way and plucks my car keys from my hand. "No driving, at least for now, Jake. The last thing you want is to have a seizure in the car."

"No driving!"

"At least until the medicine has time to take effect."

"But it only happens when I'm sleeping!"

"Just for now, Jake," she insists.

Dad, who has retreated into the den but can hear every word, says nothing. I go out into the rain-soaked yard and head toward the heavy bag Dad's hung from a tree to help me practice my shot. I lunge towards it at least twenty times, until my shoulder's sore and I'm sopping wet. Then Dad appears from out of the darkness, pulling his slicker over his shirt.

"Give her time, she'll change her mind," he says. "This is new to her. She wants to protect you."

"What am I supposed to do, let you drive me around like a ten-year-old? What about when you're working?"

"Give her a couple of days. She's blown it out of all proportion. She'll come around." He puts his hand to his hair, which is covered with a fine film of raindrops, and roots around like he's looking for cooties. "The only thing is, Jake— I wouldn't mention it to too many people. People hear a word like this—" He means *epilepsy* but doesn't say it. "They get scared. They think you can't do things. Not just driving. People think you can't do—"

"You mean they'll think I shouldn't wrestle. Like Mom was about to suggest before Dr. Symmes stopped her." I hit the bag again, then stop.

"All I'm saying is, I wouldn't make waves if I didn't have to."

"Don't worry, Dad. There's not a soul I'm planning to discuss this with. Not a soul."

• • •

I barely have time to come in and dry off before it sinks in what this means. Not telling a soul, I realize, means it's time to begin my career as The Great Liar.

Coach once advised, when Marcus was telling one of his more outrageous stories, that if you are going to lie, you ought to keep it as close to the truth as possible. "Otherwise you have to remember too many wrong details, and you'll mess it up." At the time, Coach was blowing off steam and not meaning to teach us anything useful. But when Callie calls to ask why I wasn't in school today, I remember his advice. Stay as close to the truth as possible.

"I went to the doctor," I tell her. "I had an EEG."

"An EEG!" She sounds truly alarmed. "What for?"

"Remember when I was sick? When I had such bad headaches with that flu thing? I still get them sometimes."

"I don't remember the headaches being anything special."

"I guess they weren't. They didn't find anything. No problem."

"Are you sure, Jake?"

"They gave me some pills to keep them from coming back." Brilliant, I think. If she spots my medicine, I'm set.

"Then do you want to pick me up after chorus tomorrow?"

"I wish I could," I tell her. "But I'm grounded."

"For what?"

"Mom's in one of her moods."

"I never thought of your mom as moody."

"Believe me, she is."

"Is she making you stay in this weekend?"

Uh-oh. Maybe The Great Liar needs a little practice. "She'll probably calm down by then," I say.

Callie sighs. "Oh, Jake. Your mother is the calmest person I know."

• • •

Two days pass. I take my pills. I get rides to school and home from practice. I see Callie only in the hallways. I hate every minute.

Not having a car is making me crazy. I can't concentrate on anything else. It's not only inconvenient; it's humiliating. You'd think I'd be worried about the medicine, which might make me feel strange (but hasn't so far). Or about my health and my future. But all I can think about is driving.

The next time we wrestle, I'm so busy re-living the empty feel of my hand after Mom plucked the key out of it that I don't even get nervous while I'm warming up. I do jumping jacks and watch Marcus make mincemeat out of his opponent. I tell myself, Marcus doesn't have a car. I tell myself, it doesn't bother him.

This should make me feel better, but it doesn't.

My opponent is a kid who shouldn't be able to score on me. I'm not worried even when I get out there. I take him down right off the whistle. No sweat. Once you have your own set of wheels, I think, you expect it to be a permanent thing.

Next thing I know, the kid has reversed me.

I get my act together and escape. But I'm still distracted. This is not like thinking about food when a match is going well. Then the idea takes up a small place at the edge of my mind and lets me wrestle by instinct. Now the car is taking all my concentration. At the end of first period, the score is tied. Coach gets up and holds his arms out, like, "What's wrong with you, Jake?"

I shrug and look in the other direction.

Second period I try to imagine the kid is the guy who stole my bike. I try to picture a snake slithering onto the mat. Nothing helps. I'm behind by one near the end of third period. With ten seconds to go, I take the guy down and win by a single point when it should have been at least a shut-out, if not a pin.

"Where were you tonight?" Coach asks afterwards.

"I don't know. Sorry, Coach." To my surprise, he lets it drop. I sit down and watch the other wrestlers. Brunson, our heavyweight, is back from football. Brunson doesn't have a car, I think, and his father is a dentist who can afford one. The only other senior who has a vehicle is Brian Fensel, and his is a motorcycle I truly don't envy.

But still I feel rotten.

As if he's reading my mind, Coach comes over just then. "I know you've heard me say this before, but I'm going to say it again. There are a million excuses, Jake, and half of them are legit. I don't know what's eating you and I don't care. It doesn't matter. Whatever it is, the only way you reach your potential is by blocking out your troubles and focusing on the task at hand. Every time. Regardless."

He points his finger at my face and says in his flat, scary tone, "Don't make excuses."

• • •

As it turns out, I don't have to. Everyone else is going to do it for me. Over pizza, Dad spares me his usual half-hour critique of my wrestling. He never once tells me I should have kept the underhook or that my shot was a little off. All he says is, "Don't feel bad, Jake. It's been a tough week."

"I wrestled like crap," I say.

"You won."

I look at Chopper, who says not a word. He stuffs enough pizza in his mouth to gag on, washes it down with a gallon of Pepsi, stares at his plate. He probably feels sorry for me, too.

A knot of anger forms inside my chest. This is my own kin here, and we're having a regular pity party.

"Remember when I had to have my ear drained?" I ask.

"Sure. Last winter," Dad says.

Chopper chokes down his mouthful of pizza. "You looked like hell."

This is the first note of truth all night. My cauliflower ear had formed and blossomed. The cartilage was so swollen that I winced at the slightest touch. Even my headgear wouldn't protect it. I had to let Dr. Crystal stick a needle in it and draw out the fluid, which sounds a lot worse than it actually felt. Then she wrapped my head around and around with gauze until I looked like I'd been in a major car wreck. Then Mom drove me to school.

Looking at myself in the mirror in the car, I saw the caricature of a disaster survivor, somebody wearing a bad Halloween costume. I was sure when I got to class, everybody would laugh. But they didn't. Instead, they got these serious looks on their faces as if they were worried about me and thought I couldn't handle it. And that was worse.

That day was the one and only time The Mackerel was nice to me. Her expression softened, a tiny smile turned up the corners of her mouth. "Goodness, Jake," she said, without the slightest hint of sarcasm. "You sure you're all right?" I could pinpoint the exact moment when she decided my bandages meant weakness.

Sitting in the restaurant with Chopper and Dad a whole year later, the memory still makes me mad. The knot in my chest tightens so much I have to cough to loosen it up. "My bandages might have made me look like I was hurting, but the ear was no big deal. And this is no big deal, either.

Save your pity for someone who needs it."

Dad and Chopper both stare at me. "Point well taken," Dad finally says.

"You were right," Chopper tells me. "You wrestled like crap."

But it's too late. I know when he's humoring me. If my own brother thinks I'm pitiful, what's everybody else going to think?

There's no way I'm going to live like that.

I'm going to have to be very, very careful.

The Great Liar better hone his skills.

CHAPTER 10

All week at practice, Marcus takes me down about half the time he shoots, which almost never happens. Not only am I stewing over the car, I'm also playing a new game in my head: "What will I say if?" If somebody asks about my driving, about my pills, you name it. Nothing really captures my attention until the afternoon three street guys saunter into the wrestling room and start jiving around. They're wearing loose pants that hang down around their hips and hundred-dollar sneakers probably bought with drug money.

"You gonna rassle?" one of them asks another.

"Yeah, I might. What if I rassle him?" He points to Pole, who's practicing lunges on the mat. He's about twice Pole's size.

Pole continues drilling as if he didn't hear.

"Hey, man, I was talking to you."

Pole stops but doesn't say anything. He's too busy trying not to look scared. He reminds me of myself when I was a freshman, even more afraid of those guys than he is. The would-be "rasslers" are always big and the person they want to "rassle" with is always small and frail. They'd never go after anyone like Fensel or Brunson.

The street guys laugh, and from the look on Pole's face, I figure they're joking about his strength and manhood, all in a fake-friendly way as if they expect him to laugh

about it, too. Pole stares at them and doesn't say a word.
Even in his clueless state, he knows if he laughs he'll seem
weaker.

I register all this and start in Pole's direction just as
Coach notices, too. He gets there before I do.

"How about picking on somebody more your own
size?" Coach asks the guy who's doing most of the talking.
Then he points to me. "Or if you want a little guy, how
about wrestling with Jake here?"

"Naw, man," the kid says.

"No? Why not?"

"I was just watching."

Coach catches my elbow and pulls me closer.
"You're not afraid of Jake, are you?" He arranges his face
into an expression of disbelief. "Come on. Look at him. A
skinny little fellow. You outweigh him by a ton. You ought
to be able to turn him every which way but loose."

"Naw, man," the big kid says. By this time most of
the team is watching. The guy turns to his friends, who all
laugh. Coach doesn't think it's funny.

"What's your name?" he asks.

"Gerald."

"That's what you came out here for, isn't it, Gerald?
To learn to wrestle?"

"Yeah, but I mean— I don't have no workout shorts
or nothing."

"We'll give you some. Or you can wrestle in your
clothes. Whatever you want."

By now Gerald can't gracefully refuse. Coach
guides both of us to the mat. Gerald is almost as big as
Brunson, a hulk. When I was Pole's age, I'd have been terrified of anybody who outweighed me by that much. But

now, as Coach gives Gerald a quick wrestling lesson, I'm not afraid at all – not of Gerald or his buddies, or of what might happen on the mat or any time later. "No punching," Coach tells Gerald. And he motions us to start.

Gerald never even sees me coming. The second the whistle blows I take him to his back in one swift move. Gerald's friends watch in stunned silence. Nobody told them you can be the size of Goliath and the world's greatest natural athlete too, but if you don't know the moves, anybody with experience can tear you up. When Gerald gets up and brushes himself off, everybody on the team knows neither he or his friends will cause trouble again, at least not in the wrestling room.

After they leave, Coach beckons Pole over for a talk. "You know, when those guys are in a group and they talk that trash, other kids back off, typically. But you didn't. That was smart."

"Yeah, well thanks," Pole says. One thing about Coach is, he's not afraid to tell it like it is. This is because he really doesn't care if you're from the streets or upper crust, or if you're black or white, or if you speak good English or have a heavy accent. All he cares is that, if you come into his wrestling room, you come because you want to wrestle and not because you're out to hassle somebody.

"Every year a couple of those guys come out to beat up on freshmen and intimidate them," he tells Pole. "They think they're bad-asses. But most of them are all mouth."

Coach slings a hand onto Pole's shoulder and guides him away from the rest of us. Even though they're out of earshot, I know he's giving Pole the same speech he gave me my own freshman year – and what strikes me right now is that, in the three years since, I've never heard anything like it from any other teacher. Most of them are like The Mackerel last year, who pretended everyone in AP English and every writer we studied was some neutral shade of tan who shared the same set of values and the same mother tongue. It was as if she'd decided that, in a city school like Maynard, you had to pretend skin color and where you live didn't matter.

But sometimes you think those things are all that *do* matter. Like freshman year when two big losers came after me in the wrestling room and left me feeling so ashamed that by the time practice ended, I was seriously thinking about quitting.

"I'll tell you something, Jake," Coach had said then, squeezing my shoulder exactly the way he's squeezing Pole's right now. "Except for Thompson, not one kid who's ever come in off the street like that has ever had the guts to stick around. Except for Thompson, not one of them ever had the balance you have. Or the raw talent. If you stay with it and work hard, before long you'll be tearing them up. But you have to work."

Thompson was our top wrestler then, so I was flattered, and *raw talent* was a sweet phrase to hear. But mainly the idea of someday tearing up those bullies who'd humiliated me so badly – or at least knowing I could – was strong motivation. As they say, the rest is history.

I watch Pole on the other side of the wrestling room with Coach, looking interested and hopeful. I think he's going to be okay. This is not politically correct to talk about, but the core of our team this year is me, who's white; Marcus, who's "ghetto black" and has what The Mackerel would term a whole different "ethnic heritage"; and Brunson, who's black but whose "heritage" is closer to mine than to Marcus's, since his parents live together, his father practices dentistry, and no one in his family sells illegal drugs. If we pretended there were no differences on the wrestling team, we'd probably kill each other.

Coach finishes his speech and claps Pole on the back to send him off. Pole comes toward us standing a lot straighter and looking a lot prouder than he did before. For a second I feel grateful all over again that the sick fear those fast-talking thugs used to put in me is a thing of the past. And not just because I've gotten to know guys like Marcus, but because I know I can handle any of them that come along. Because deep down, I'm a bad-ass, too.

Which is what I think Coach was trying to remind me when he picked me to take that kid down.

For the rest of the day, I wrestle the way I used to. I forget about the car. I forget about lying to Callie. I stub out the smolder in my mind and focus, focus, focus.

* * *

Later, I find myself outside the gym with only Wanda Custer for company. Dad's late, and everyone else has left.

Wanda's hair has always been cut into short spikes, but this week she's added two streaks of color to the front – one orange and one purple. She looks ridiculous.

"That was neat," she tells me as she hikes her backpack to her shoulder. "Your taking up for Pole like that." Great. Now we're going to have to have a conversation. The good mood I had at the end of practice crumbles into dust.

"It was Coach's idea for me to wrestle," I say. "I didn't have a choice."

"Yeah, but it proved the point. I mean, you know—The team supporting new kids, like him and me."

I can't believe she's putting herself in the same category with Pole. It annoys me even to be standing here with her.

"You know what the difference is between you and Pole?" I ask her. "The difference is, you come to practice whenever you feel like it and he comes every day. The difference is, he's working his butt off and you're playing games."

"Yeah, right. I come out here for you guys to dump on me because I'm a masochist."

"You said it, not me." I walk toward the curb, look down the block for cars. Nothing.

Wanda follows me. "I'm not a masochist," she says.

"An attention-freak, then. The girl who wants her picture in the yearbook with her rainbow hair and a quote about being Maynard's first woman wrestler."

"A quote in the yearbook!"

"Well?" I raise my eyebrows at her. The Great Liar might have to keep his dirty secret about his fits, but in some respects he's brutally honest.

"You're not out for pure love of the sport, that's for sure," I tell her. "If you were you'd be coming to practice every day. You'd be running and lifting weights. You'd be doing the things everybody else does to get in shape."

Wanda lifts her hand to the purple streak in her hair, as if the insult's just sunk in. She hikes her backpack higher. Her nostrils flare. "You're not wrestling so hot lately yourself, Mr. Pure Love of the Sport," she snaps.

Touché.

"Sometimes," I tell her, "I look at you and think,

'This person wrestles so badly, she must be suffering from more than simple inexperience. She must be sick or something.' Are you?"

"No. Of course not."

I'm aware that this is getting out of hand, but I don't stop.

"What I ask myself is, why is she out for wrestling, anyway? She's not even a freshman, she's a junior. Everybody knows wrestling takes a couple of years to learn. So what's the point? Is she glad she's doing it? She doesn't look like she is." I'm in her face now, but she doesn't back off. "Well, are you glad? Are you?"

"No," she says. "If you want to know the truth, no." She shifts the backpack again and gives me a glacial glare.

I take another look down street for cars. What's taking Dad so long? Why am I standing here with this clueless girl instead of driving myself home? She comes up to me and half-pokes, half-punches me in the arm.

"You don't know as much as you think," she says.

"No?"

"No."

"Like what?"

She freezes. Looks scared.

"What?" I repeat. I'm losing patience.

"Like Coach," she mumbles.

The Great Liar knows when someone's trying to change the subject, but still it makes me mad. "Coach! If you've got problems, Wanda, don't blame Coach."

"He'd like me to quit coming to practice, don't tell me he wouldn't."

"You think so? When Marcus first came out for wrestling, he was like one of those guys going after Pole today. He was a pain in the ass. You think Coach drove him away?   No.   He paid to get him his physical so he could play sports."

"Very magnanimous."

"He buys kids wrestling shoes. He helps them get jobs so they can raise money for wrestling camp. He doesn't drive them away."   Which now that I think of it, even in Wanda's case, is true.

"That's not it, anyway," she says. "It's—" She stops.

"Listen, if you're going to share some deep secret here, either spill it or don't."

The way she looks at me, you'd think I'd slapped her.

Then her mother drives up. Wanda opens the door and slings her backpack into the seat. She raises her hand to cover the streaks in her hair so I can't see them while she gets into the car.

I'm left standing on the curb, feeling like a jerk for making her want to hide her hair. Even when you're hurting, Jake boy, I tell myself, it's wrong to take it out on someone else.

CHAPTER 11

Next thing I know, it's Thanksgiving. When you wrestle, usually the worst thing about the holidays is that you can't pig out because you're in the middle of the season. But this time it's more than food. It's Mom.

She comes home on Wednesday and goes into her wholesome meals routine, something we haven't seen since the Big Career Move. She sends Dad out for cranberries; she starts chopping celery and onions for stuffing. She makes two pumpkin pies and two apple, and right before bed she puts the turkey in the oven so that we smell it roasting all night. When I come down in the morning, she's already peeling potatoes, wearing a frilly apron over her sweats. We should nominate her for Mother of the Year.

She doesn't say good morning. She doesn't say Happy Thanksgiving. First words out of her mouth are, "Don't forget your medicine, Jake."

"I've been taking it every day, Mom."

"I know." But she watches me down the pills.

Aunt Kaye and Uncle Barney show up at noon with my cousin Timmy and a sweet potato casserole with at least a thousand calories per spoonful. I don't even look at it, much less eat it. Forty-eight hours from now, I have to make weight. We're wrestling at the Eagle's Ridge Tournament on Saturday, against some of the best teams in the state. Coach is pretty sure Colby Douglas will be there, the guy who beat me by two points at regionals last year. I'm ready to find out how good he is this year. When the turkey goes around for seconds, I pass.

I turn down ice cream with my pumpkin pie. I chew slowly. Coach likes to say the Thanksgiving tournaments separate the men from the boys. If you pig out on Thursday and Friday and don't make weight on Saturday, you're a boy. If you control yourself, you're a man.

After we do the dishes, Chopper and I take our cousin Timmy into the yard and throw a football around long enough to burn a couple hundred calories. Later, I run three miles. I don't eat anything else all day. When Callie and I go to a movie that night with Steven Wills and his girl-friend, driving's not an issue because Steven takes his car, and the hardest thing I have to do is pass up the popcorn. Mom's waiting when I get in. "Good movie?" she asks cheerily.

"It was okay."

"Well, goodnight. Don't forget your pill."

"Already took it." I restrain myself from saying a whole lot more.

Friday morning there's a short practice at school to help us drop weight. I'm a couple of pounds up, but I can take it off by tomorrow. When I get home, Mom and Dad are in the den watching football on TV. It's cozy but also weird. Until the Big Career Move, Mom never watched football or any other sport. When Chopper and I were younger, she came to our soccer and baseball games to show her support, but she never understood what was going on. After watching me get thumped my first freshman wrestling match, she was almost in tears, which is unusual for her. "I know you're trying hard and I'm proud of you,

Jake," she said. "But I'm not sure I can stand to watch you get thrown around like that." She didn't come to another match until last year, when I was doing the throwing. The point is, she's not a sports fan. So why the sudden interest in football?

Well, I know: It's guilt. Before the Big Career Move, when she was cooking meals and staying at home, everything was okay. Now she's gone and Jake has a brain disorder. She feels responsible.

I go into the kitchen, open the refrigerator, survey the contents. The leftover turkey is piled on a plate and covered with plastic wrap; ditto for stuffing, cranberry sauce, apple pie. Chopper reaches around me and lifts out a piece of pie like it's a cookie. I curb my impulse to slam the refrigerator door on his hand.

"It's a good thing Coach Lindy doesn't like his wrestlers going down two or three weight classes. You'd never make it." Chopper stuffs pie into his mouth. One gooey piece escapes and lands on the red, white, and blue Marine Corps design on his T-shirt.

"Slob," I say.

"Oh, man, it's Grumpus," he tells me as he rubs apple into his shirt.

"You try not eating sometime, smart-ass." The truth is, Chopper could go for days without food and never notice as long as his computer was working.

He rubs the shirt some more. The caption running across it reads, "These colors don't run." He finally gives up, lifts his finger to his mouth, and licks it.

"Gross, Chopper."

"You're just jealous. Grumpus better take a chill pill before I come over there and beat his butt."

"In your next life, little brother."

Mom comes into the kitchen with a big smile on her face, as if she hasn't heard us bickering. "I'm making myself a turkey sandwich. How about some lunch?"

"I'm a couple pounds over," I grumble. *Doesn't she know this?*

"Something small, then? To take when you take the medication?"

"You don't have to take the pills with food. Besides, I don't take another pill until dinnertime. I can handle it. We're into major over-reaction here, Mom."

"Turkey sounds good," Chopper says. "With mayonnaise and a slice of cheese."

After he eats, Chopper locks himself in with the computer to avoid me until I leave for Eagle's Ridge. To tell the truth, I can't blame him.

We go to out-of-town tournaments the night before so we can run or work out before weigh-ins the next morning. Since the wrestling budget is minuscule compared to the football budget, we stay in the most fleabag motels imaginable, sometimes half the team in a single room. This time I only have to share a room with the other seniors – Marcus, Brian Fensel, and Brunson.

Marcus and I take one of the double beds, which isn't ideal but isn't bad, either, since we're about the same size. We let Fensel fight with Brunson over the other bed. Considering Brunson weighs 235 and Fensel 160, Fensel finally opts to sleep on the floor.

Marcus' mother has promised to come watch the next day, so he's in a relatively peaceful mood. We go out to run, then listen to Coach's usual pep talk and the empty rumbling of our stomachs (except for Brunson, who as heavyweight gets to eat as much as he wants). We watch TV for a while and finally hit the sack. I take my pills the last time I go into the bathroom, then slip them into my jeans' pocket. If somebody sees them, I'll say they're for allergies.

Marcus and I have had to sleep together in these motel rooms so many times that we have a system. We turn our backs to each other; we try not to hog the space. If one of us wakes up too close to center, we skootch over and shove the other one over, too. The last thing either of us wants is to find ourselves touching or (ugh) tangled up.

In about two seconds, Marcus is out cold. But not me. Glad as I am to have escaped Mom's hovering, I can't help wondering if she's still playing Mother of the Year at home now that I'm gone and don't have to be coddled. Chopper's her baby, but somehow I have the idea the ten thousand Thanksgiving dishes and cozy scene watching football with Dad were for my benefit and not his. To show me how "normal" things are despite my recent medical problems. The whole idea makes me mad.

Then another awful thought strikes: What if I fall asleep and *something happens?* Marcus would be freaked out. But having Brunson and Brian Fensel see me have a fit would be worse. In ten seconds the whole school would know. The only way to prevent it is to stay awake.

As soon as I resolve to do this, I fall asleep and don't wake up until morning. And everything's all right.

We all make weight without any trouble. The only surprise is, Colby Douglas isn't anywhere to be seen. His coach says his family is away for the holiday. I'm disappointed and relieved, too. I've brought both my lucky workout shirts – Bad to the Bone and the tie-dye shirt Callie gave me for my birthday. Callie's shirt is shades of red and pink, something I would have called a wuss shirt at one time but have convinced myself I'm man enough to wear. One of Life's Little Tests. So far, I've never lost when I wore it. Never lost with Bad to the Bone, either.

I'm pleased at how well the day goes. Every match, I'm aware of how much stronger and smoother I am than I was a couple of weeks ago, even with everything that's happened in between. It might be a gray, cold day outside, and back home Mom might be in Domestic Servant mode, but for a couple of hours inside this too-warm gym, things feel completely normal. I win my weight class with only one tough match in the finals. Marcus would win, too, except that Lizard Smith's at the tournament – a kid who's already won the state three times and is likely to be one of the few guys ever to be a state champion all his four years of high school. Knowing how good Lizard is, Marcus is proud of himself for not getting pinned with his mama looking on, so he doesn't pull a single stunt the whole time we're having dinner after the meet or riding back on the bus.

We don't get back to town until one-thirty in the morning. Mom, the early-to-bed lady, is still awake. She pretends she's anxiously waiting to hear how I've done, but sports-fan Dad is in bed already, so it's pretty obvious her real motive is to watch me take my medicine. If I weren't so tired, I'd give her a piece of my mind.

I'm both glad and sorry I didn't when, the next morning, I sleep until eleven-thirty and Mom insists she'll make me pancakes for breakfast even though everyone else ate hours ago.

"I thought you like to relax on Sunday," I say. "Besides, you have to get your stuff ready to go, don't you?"

"I know how hard it was for you, not being able to eat all weekend," she replies.

"I could get something. I wouldn't starve."

She sets syrup on the table and hands me a plate. "You want milk or water?"

"Water's the beverage of choice during wrestling season."

She laughs as if I've said something funny.

Afterwards, Mom and Dad watch the news shows together. Usually it's Dad watching the news and Mom in the other room doing the Sunday crossword. We're pretending it's business as usual, we're playing House – big meals, special attentions, intimate family moments. What a crock.

Finally, about four o'clock, she packs her suitcase for the week.

"Don't forget your medicine, Jake," she tells me as she gets into her car.

"Don't worry. I'm not three years old anymore."

"Good." She flashes me a winning smile as she pulls out of the driveway.

When the car finally disappears around the corner, it's the first time I feel like I can breathe.

CHAPTER 12

I tell Callie Mom wants to have the brakes on her car fixed and in the meantime doesn't think it's safe for me to drive. Very close to the truth, the last part anyway. The Great Liar gets smoother every day.

The next time Dad works evenings, Callie's waiting for me outside practice in her mother's Dodge Spirit. First thing she does is turn off the ignition and get out. Maybe it's to satisfy my macho pride or maybe it's stupid, but whenever she picks me up to go somewhere, she always lets me drive.

She's expecting me to do that now.

I open the door and throw my wrestling gear in the back seat. There's no reason I shouldn't drive. I'm wide awake. I've got the pills in my pocket. I've been on the medicine plenty of time for it to "take effect." Nothing's going to happen.

But an odd thing does. Instead of getting into the driver's seat, I hesitate. I meant to bring up the driving issue with Mom over the weekend, but it never happened. For about the millionth time I rerun her plucking my keys out of my hand. I feel the itchy emptiness in my fingers. And yet *I feel honor-bound to obey her.*

As if it's coming from somewhere outside of me, I hear The Great Liar say, "You drive, Callie. I'm beat. It was a hell of a practice."

"You sure?"

"Yeah. Go ahead." I get into the passenger side and buckle my seat belt. She slips into the driver's seat and regards me quizzically.

"You sure?" she asks again.

"Sure. Go ahead," I repeat.

She turns the key in the ignition. "Are you all right, Jake?"

"Yeah, just tired," The Great Liar says.

"You don't have one of those headaches?"

There are no headaches, I want to tell her. "No. I'm fine."

"You sure?"

If she says, "you sure" once more, I'm going to explode.

• • •

We buy take-out sandwiches and bring them back to the house. Dad's working tonight; Mom's away. I'm in a rotten mood, wondering what I've become that I'm afraid to drive a car just because my mother tells me not to. The Great Liar turned Goody-Goody.

"Chopper, we brought supper!" I yell when we get into the house. He comes down from his computer, but his mind is still in cyberspace. He doesn't even tell Callie hello.

"You care if I take this upstairs?" He grabs a sandwich and a napkin. "I have a million hours of work to do."

"No. Fine. Go earn your fortune." Actually, I'm relieved. If we all had to sit around the table together, no telling what he might say about you-know-what. But this is his busy time of year, when he does research for people whose term papers are due before Christmas. He doesn't write their papers (Mom would kill him), but he searches databases on any given subject and prints out relevant articles for a price. He makes more money than any other fourteen-year-old I know.

"Jake, you're a million miles away," Callie says when she finishes her sandwich. "Do you think they'll buy a raffle ticket or not?"

"Who?" I realize I've been watching the doorway for the USMC bulldog on Chopper's shirt, afraid he'll come back downstairs.

"Your Dad. Do you think he'll buy a ticket for the chorus fund-raiser? It's a color TV."

"Yeah, sure." The chorus fund-raiser. The chorus is raising money for a competition over the holidays. They'll be gone three or four days, I can't remember, competing against singers from all over the country. Callie's all keyed up about it, but to me, it sounds trivial compared to my last couple of weeks. Not that she has any way of knowing that. "Dad's good for at least a couple of tickets," I tell her. "He's a real sucker for fund-raisers."

"Jake, what's wrong with you?"

"Nothing. Why?"

"You make it sound like some kind of rip-off."

"Don't be so sensitive, Callie." I grab the wrappers from the sandwiches we've just finished, crumple them into a ball, aim them at the trash can.

"I'm not being sensitive." Callie gets up, tosses her hair, heads into the den. "You've been acting weird all day."

I don't care if she leaves. Maybe it would be better. But I follow her, and when she bends over to pick up her coat from the couch, I brush her hair out of the way and kiss her neck. "There's nothing wrong with me," I croon into her ear. "I think I was just hungry."

She hesitates, not sure if she wants to forgive me. Then she turns around and opens her arms to me. "You're always hungry during wrestling season," she whispers.

We end up on the couch in front of the TV. Compared to most couples we know, our physical relationship is in the rudimentary stages. Callie always has her sister's pregnancy in the back of her mind and isn't about to let things go too far. Although nothing more happens than usual, by the time Callie decides she'd better go, I've realized an important fact. Dr. Symmes is right: the medicine is not going to affect my sex life. Given the opportunity, impotence would certainly not be a problem.

• • •

Chopper comes downstairs half an hour later. "I did some research on your condition," he says.

"Why? Somebody writing a term paper about it?"

"I'm tired of not having you as my chauffeur."

"Ah."

"The way I see it is, you ought to be able to drive. Considering that you only have nocturnal seizures."

"Nocturnal seizures," I repeat. He looks so serious that I can't help clowning. "Similar to nocturnal ejaculations?"

"Yeah, but not as much fun."

"How do you know about nocturnal seizures?"

"The Web," he says.

"The Web!" I have visions of him broadcasting my problem over the Internet, posting the details on his Web site, asking for feedback. Finally he grins.

"Some people with nocturnal seizures never even

know about it unless somebody tells them," he says. "They wake up in the morning and their sheets are all rumpled from thrashing around, but that's all they know."

He motions me to follow him upstairs to the computer.

"A lot of people only have problems within an hour of going to sleep or waking up. Never during the day," he says as he sits down in front of the screen. "It's pretty common."

"Far as I can tell, since I've been on this medicine I've had no problems at all, little bro."

"Which makes it even better." He begins to push his glasses up, but for once, they haven't slid down. I notice that somehow, all of a sudden, his nose isn't nonexistent anymore. It's grown to an almost normal size. Big enough to hold his glasses. I stare at him. How could this have happened?

He doesn't see me gaping because he's busy typing something. A colorful chart pops up on the computer screen. "See?" I stare at rows of statistics about epileptics with nocturnal seizures. "If you can pretty much count on no seizures unless you're asleep or close to it, they ought to let you drive."

A thin ray of hope blooms in my chest. "Especially now that I'm on the medicine."

Chopper prints out the chart and hands it to me. "Dad'll buy it, for sure," he says. "I wouldn't be so sure about Mom."

And of course he's right.

• • •

Dad brings it up on Saturday, after he's already

given me permission to drive as long as Mom agrees. As always when trouble looms, serenity settles over her like a cloud.

"I thought we agreed he wouldn't take the car until the medicine took effect," she says to Dad in her annoyingly calm and reasonable voice.

"It's had plenty of time to get in my system," I interrupt. "You know it has. I've had no problems. None."

She folds her arms in front of her, fixes me with a level gaze. "I think we should wait through New Year's."

"Why?"

"Just to be safe."

"If you really want to be safe, why not wait till Easter? Why not the fourth of July?" Mom doesn't want me to get hurt, wants me to be "all right," but as far as I can tell, she doesn't care if that means living in a cage.

"He's right, Diane," Dad says. "It makes no sense to keep him waiting. The date is arbitrary."

"No, it's not. According to the Department of Motor Vehicles, you're supposed to be seizure-free for a year before you drive."

"You called the DMV?" I gasp.

"I didn't tell them."

"I've done a little checking of my own," Dad says. "Officially, you're supposed to tell the Department of Motor Vehicles if you've been diagnosed with epilepsy, but the law doesn't say when. Most people wait until it's time to renew their license. In the meantime they monitor themselves. They don't drive if the medicine doesn't control their seizures. Nobody wants to kill themselves – or somebody else."

"You can't be sure—" she begins. I hand her the

chart Chopper printed out. She frowns.

Mothers see things at the lowest common denominator. They want you to be "all right," but they don't understand that what makes you "all right" is the life you lead – like wrestling or having a girlfriend. Or driving a car.

"You know how Jake got home from school yesterday?" Chopper asks her. "On Brian Fensel's motorcycle. Which do you think is safer? That – or driving home himself?"

She blanches. "You rode on the motorcycle?"

"Brian lent me his extra helmet."

"Jake's seventeen," Dad tells her. "He's at the age when he's supposed to be taking more responsibility, not less. Shutting him down when he's responding perfectly well—"

"It's risky," she whispers.

"Everything is risky," Dad says. "Life is risky."

She stands rigid, hands on her hips.

"Listen," Dad says, "let's get back to what we know. We know Jake had two or three seizures all in about a week, and we know that since he's been on medicine he hasn't had any more. We know people with nocturnal seizures often don't have any other kind. We know he wants to drive, and we know life around here will be more convenient if he does." The way Dad lists these things, he sounds more like Mom than he does like himself, calm and sensible. She looks up and listens.

"Okay," she says finally.

"Okay what?"

"You can drive. But if there are any more problems . . . even a hint of one, you have to promise—"

"I promise, Mom."

"You're taking on a big responsibility. I need to know I can trust you."

"Don't worry, Mom, you can."

• • •

Driving again is paradise. I take Callie to chorus. Pick her up. Hardly notice that we don't have as much to say to each other now that I have to censor everything that comes out of my mouth. I figure lying will get easier with time. I drive to the Y. I drive to practice. For the first time ever, I actually enjoy filling the tank with gas. I actually enjoy taking Chopper to Discount Computer to buy a new Zip drive with all the money he's earned. When he gets back into the car and says, "Onward, Jacob," as if I'm his chauffeur, I refrain from pulverizing him.

He's still in his manic mood when we get home. He's always this way when his geekhead habit has been fed.

He takes the Zip drive out of its box and holds it up in admiration. "I sure am glad we solved your driving problem," he says, "because the scholarship's going to be a bummer."

A bummer? The scholarship is one of the best things that's happened to me all year. I figure he must be joking.

CHAPTER 13

"What *about* my scholarship?" I demand.

Chopper gets a kind of strangled, puzzled expression on his face.

"Losing it, I mean."

"Losing it. Very funny, Chopper."

He turns his attention to some wires that connect the Zip drive to the computer. He won't look up. "Come on, Jake. Don't tell me you didn't know."

"Know what? You have a sick sense of humor."

"I'm not trying to make jokes. I thought you knew."

"Knew *what?*" I ask again.

When his attention shifts from the Zip drive to my face, he looks like a spotlighted deer, wide-eyed and frozen. "You can't be in the military if you have epilepsy," he finally blurts. "You have to be— you know, not dependent on medicine."

I lean against the door, let this sink in. I don't understand.

"So you could fight under any conditions, anywhere in the world," Chopper explains. "Even if you couldn't get your pills."

He clears his throat; he's having trouble getting the words out. "If you go five years with no seizures and no medication, then they'll consider you," he whispers.

"But not now?"

"No." The Zip drive lies abandoned on his desk. His post-shopping glow has faded. "I'm sorry," he says. "I thought you knew."

"I never thought about it till now." I'm still leaning against the door. My body feels too heavy to move. My mind has gone eerily blank.

"Jake, I really thought you knew," Chopper says again. His voice cracks a little. He looks like he's about to cry.

"It's okay," I tell him. "It's not your fault."

I go into my room and sit on my bed. My mind's a gray slate, numb and so quiet it's almost like pain. Down the hall, Chopper puts on a Shania Twain CD. Although I hear it, the sound doesn't penetrate. I'm alone inside the aching silence.

After a while I go over to my dresser and open my T-shirt drawer. The one on top is black with white lettering. It says, "If it Absolutely, Positively, Has to Be Destroyed Overnight: U.S. Marines."

Destroyed overnight. I know just how it feels.

I take all the Marine Corps T-shirts out of my drawer and put them on top of the dresser. There must be a dozen of them that Dad has given me for every birthday and every Christmas I can remember. They're jumbled and wrinkled, but I fold each one and stack them in a neat pile. Then I carry them into the computer room and set them on Chopper's desk.

"Present for you," I say.

He looks worried. "Where are you going?"

"To lift weights," I tell him. Even when life sucks, you can still get big as hell.

• • •

At the Y, I make my way back to the weight room, glad to see it's nearly empty. Then I see why: a girl. Lifting the smallest possible dumbbells over in the corner. Nobody likes to share the room with a girl.

I back out before she can see me, before I really see her. Whoever she is, she picked a choice time to come here. Usually women prefer the Nautilus room with its fancy machines and mirrors. The free weight room is old and basic, nothing but weights, benches, pull-up bars, and a rotting wood floor that buckles in places where the roof leaks. Except for a few serious-weightlifter women who know what they're doing, the free weight room is strictly a male hangout where you can grunt or spit or fart and no one will care.

What I want to do right now is curse and howl and get rid of this silent ache that takes over when the future collapses in front of you.

The last thing I want to do is make small-talk with some girl.

• • •

I drive around for nearly an hour. It's a clear night, cold, with a million stars out, a few clouds scudding across a three-quarter moon. Without realizing it, I head toward Callie's. I'm within a block when I think: if I see her, what will I say? You can't tell someone the splinter's beginning to fester if you've never told them about the splinter.

I'm hungry but don't want to eat. Heading toward the Interstate, I step on the gas and open the window, let the cold wind come rushing in. It drowns out the silence inside my head, it makes my face tingle, my fingers sting. This is better. My mind's blank, the ache is gone. Then from nowhere comes a flashback to the girl in the weight room, and even though I hardly looked at her, I know now who she was.

Wanda Custer.

Probably lifting weights because I told her if she was serious about wrestling, she'd get in shape.

Not only am I a freak. I'm also creating a Frankenstein.

She'll probably never miss a wrestling practice again.

Any other time, I'd think it was funny.

At the next exit I get off the Interstate, turn around, head back to town. I'm starving. It's late. My usual fast-food stops are closed. I pull in at Benny's Always, the all-night diner, and order a bowl of chili. Beans run through your system fast, don't put on weight. Just my luck, the place is empty except for Zane Dennis, my smoker/doper neighbor and fellow senior, bottom of the graduating class. He comes over when I'm half finished and asks for a ride home.

"How'd you get here, Zane?" For all I know, he has a buddy waiting in the parking lot. Seventeen years old and his brain is so fried he might not remember.

"Brenda," he says, naming his girlfriend. "We had—" He claws the air as if searching for words. "—an altercation, man. She split."

I finish my chili, pay the check, motion Zane toward the car. We're not even out of the parking lot when he offers me a joint. "No thanks," I say.

"Not fond of the weed?"

"No, Zane."

"Wrestling season, huh? Got to stay clean." He

shakes his head as if to sympathize.

"You wouldn't know the first thing about it, Zane. There are other kinds of pleasures."

"Yeah?" He pulls a plastic baggie from a pocket, filled with pills in a rainbow of colors. "Uppers. Help you cut weight."

"Thanks. My weight's okay."

"Downers, then." He pulls a couple of capsules out of another pocket. "Keep you from getting nervous." He grins. He's hamming it up. Tempting the Jock. It's a game. We've played it before. For all I know, we're looking at an assortment of vitamins.

"You still going out with Callie Harris?" he asks.

He knows I am. He's seen us at school. I don't say anything; I'm not in the mood for this. He nods his head as if I've answered and takes some little white pills from the baggie. They look exactly like aspirin.

"Roofies," he says. "Maybe just what you need."

"I don't think we're communicating here, Zane," I tell him.

"Dissolve real easy in a drink," he says, fingering a couple of the pills. "In a beer, soda, anything."

I turn on the radio, switch to the classical music station Mom leaves in memory. The shock of hearing a string quartet might shut him up.

It doesn't.

"You put one of these in somebody's drink, half an hour later they're out cold," he says. "Next day they don't remember a thing." He grins. "Slip one of these to Callie, you could slip her something else after a while and she'd be in no position to refuse, you know what I mean?"

All at once the gray slate in my mind lights up, takes

on fiery color. I slam on the brakes, pull up to the curb. I reach over and open Zane's door.

"Out," I tell him.

"Why?"

"Out, Zane. I'm doing the rest of this trip solo."

"It's only a couple of blocks, man."

I unbuckle his seat belt, give him a little nudge. "Out," I say.

He doesn't have any choice, so he goes.

• • •

Dad's waiting for me when I get in. Not a good sign. It's a school night, it's late; he's probably figuring I had a seizure and wrecked the car. I steel myself for the lecture.

Instead he hands me a pile of the T-shirts I gave to Chopper. "I wouldn't give up on these just yet."

"No? Why not?"

He motions me to sit down. "You know, in the Marines you need 20/20 vision to go to flight school. If your vision isn't perfect the day before you start, your flying career is over. But here's the thing: if they find out the day *after* you start school, they deal with it. Maybe you can't fly front seat, but you can fly. You know what I'm saying?"

"No."

"Listen Jake, I think this thing is a fluke. I do. When I was talking to Mom about your driving, it didn't just apply to that. All your problems came in about a week's time – and ever since, nothing. We don't know whether that's because of the medicine or because of . . . who knows? I think it's going to go away. Maybe already has. I think you ought to wait before you rearrange your life because of it."

"You mean take the military physical and not tell them about the seizures?"

"The physical isn't until next summer. I mean wait and see."

He means lie.

His face is pale, almost gray.

This isn't like him.

Then I see what's going on. This is *his dream* I'm losing. His dream as much as mine.

For a second, I feel sorry for him. Then I don't. I might not be there when this so-called brain disorder comes calling, but all the same it's wrecking my life. My life, not his. Why should we pretend it isn't?

"Don't kid yourself, Dad," I say. And I drop the T-shirts into a jumble on the floor.

CHAPTER 14

As she promised, Mom works in town the last weeks before Christmas, but this turns out to be a mixed blessing. One of the Christmas presents Chopper's been promised is a pair of contact lenses. Mom wants to go with him to our regular eye doctor for his fitting. But twice they have to break his appointment because she's tied up at work. A lot of the bank staff takes off this time of year. She's running one branch office and helping at another. When Chopper tries to reschedule his eye appointment for the third time, they tell him the office will be shut all through the holidays.

"I'd have the lenses two weeks by now if it weren't for you!" he accuses Mom. "You told me I'd have them before Mona's party." This is some holiday event he's been invited to – which is saying a lot, since Chopper isn't what you'd call a party kind of guy.

"Chopper, I'm sorry, but I have to work," Mom says.

"The Vision Center at the mall stays open late. We could go there."

"I told you before – no."

"Why not?"

"Because Dr. Beckley has always tested your eyes. I trust him. You don't take chances when it comes to your vision."

"Everybody I know goes to the Vision Center. None of them are walking around blind."

"You've been wearing glasses for five years. What difference does a few more weeks make?"

He picks up the newspaper from the table and slams it down. "You know what your problem is? Your problem is, you don't even live here anymore but you still want to call all the shots!"

Mom narrows her eyes, speaks softly. "Of course I live here."

"Yeah. You come home two days a week and think you can run everything like before. Now you're working in town a couple of weeks and we're supposed to pretend you were never away. It's not normal!"

She picks up the newspaper he's slammed onto the table and sets it on a chair. "I used to think you missed having me around," she says in her low voice. "Now I realize that what you miss is having somebody provide services for you. Not just take you to the eye doctor, but take you exactly when you want to go."

She gets such a self-righteous look on her face that it makes me mad. When she left at the end of every weekend and expected us to take care of the house, she certainly wanted services from *us*. Anyway, what *is* one person's worth to another, if not something they can provide? You want to be with someone because they do something for you or are nice to you, or because you like the way they look. It's never a hundred percent unselfish.

"You promised him, Mom," I tell her. "If you can't take him, I will."

"He's under age and so are you. He needs a parent to give him permission to buy the lenses."

"Write him a note," I say.

She ignores this and looks at Chopper as if she's seeing him for the first time. "You know, when I originally took this new job, I did it for the money," she says. "But now . . . I like my job. I do. That isn't a crime."

It's the first time she's admitted this. In a way, it clears the air. In some ways, we like her job, too. Or at least I do. I like freedom I have when she isn't there.

"You say I'm not acting normal," she tells him. "Well, I am. This is normal now. It's different, but it's normal. Do you understand that?"

Chopper just stares at her.

"Normal changes," she says.

Chopper glares.

"Circumstances might change," I point out. "Normal doesn't change."

Mom regards me guiltily. Talk about changing circumstances! Perfect health one day, epilepsy the next. Scholarship winner one day, loser the next. It's the way I live now. Maybe for a long time.

But it isn't normal.

• • •

The remarkable thing about Christmas morning isn't what's in the packages we open but what isn't. Specifically, no Marine Corps T-shirts. Not for me, not for Chopper.

I get, among other things, a wrestling shirt that says "Takedown, No Sweat." Chopper gets one that reads, "Computer Nerd, and Proud of It." But there is nothing military among our loot. Nothing. The closest we come is the sweatshirt Chopper opens with a drawing of the TV-6 helicopter on the back – the one that reports on the rush hour traffic, distinctly un-warlike.

Even this strikes me as odd. Although Chopper got

his nickname when he was little because he went around the house making whump-whump helicopter noises and (best we could tell) trying to *become* a helicopter, he gave this up around the age of six. As we open one package and then another, I get the distinct feeling that everyone is trying too hard. Even Chopper and I haven't picked out the right gifts. We've pitched in to get Mom some new luggage for her traveling – as a sort of peace offering, I guess – but when she first looks at it, before she composes her face to thank us, she looks a little puzzled, a little hurt.

• • •

Callie spends Christmas at her grandmother's, but the next night I take her out to dinner. The meal, along with the kind of stupid-looking stuffed animal she likes so much, is my Christmas present to her. I plan to give her the package at the table, but when I pull into the restaurant lot, she takes a box out of a bag she's brought with her and says, "Here, Jake, open this now."

It's a T-shirt. White, with a gold globe and anchor on the front, with the eagle sitting on top of the globe. Above that, in big black letters, your typical Marine Corps slogan: BE AFRAID. And in a black box with glowing red letters: BE VERY AFRAID.

To tell the truth, I am.

"I thought it would be a good workout shirt," Callie says tentatively. By her tone, I sense I'm not showing the proper enthusiasm.

"Yeah, it's great." I check the shirt's tags in the glow of the street lights. "Hundred percent cotton, just what I like. Thanks, Cal."

"You don't like it, do you?"

"Sure I do," The Great Liar says.

She frowns. Before she can speak, I hand her the box with the stuffed animal. "Here."

She takes a long time unwrapping it. Folds the paper into a neat square. Makes a ball of the ribbon. Slowly lifts the top of the box. "Oh, a koala bear!" Holding it to her face, she caresses the phony fur. "Oh, Jake, I love it!"

Inside the restaurant, we order steaks and go to the salad bar, where Callie puts a couple of beet slices on top of her lettuce. No tomatoes, no cucumber, just beets. A twinge of irritation stabs at me. Who eats beets in their salad?

Why should I care?

The waitress brings us a miniature loaf of bread set on its own wooden tray. Callie picks up the knife to slice it, and that's when I notice her fingernails.

Among her other good qualities, Callie has nice nails. Sort of a medium length, filed to little points that make you notice how long and white and slender her fingers are. But tonight the nails are red.

Shiny. Bright. Odd-looking.

"Earth to Jake," she says.

"Huh?"

"I was telling you about the singing competition." Having raised enough money for their trip, the Maynard Singers leave tomorrow to compete against the best high school choruses in the country.

"You polished your nails," I say.

She pauses a second, realizes we're on a new sub-ject, brightens. "What do you think?" She waves her fin-gers in the air.

"They look different."

"I can take it off if you don't like it. It was just an experiment."

"Why? If you like your nails the color of fresh blood, don't let me stop you."

"If it bothers you— "

"No. Don't cave in and go back to pink just to please somebody else."

"Fine. I won't. Blood red it is." Her tone is defiant but her face is getting splotchy."

"Hey, I'm sorry." Splotches precede tears, not something I'm prepared to deal with. "All I meant was, if you like something, you don't need to change it because of me."

Callie stabs a piece of lettuce, stained pink from the beet juice. She concentrates intently on her salad plate.

"C'mon, Callie. I didn't mean anything. This is our big night out. We're supposed to be having a good time."

Nothing.

"This is costing me a fortune." Little joke.

She looks up. "Ever since you opened that T-shirt," she says, "you've been acting like I handed you a poisonous snake or something."

"I didn't mean to. I told you the T-shirt is fine."

"You would have told me a pair of piranhas was fine."

A wave of irritation passes over me. I'm tired of humoring her. "What did you want me to do? Jump up and down? Do a couple of back flips?"

She puts down her fork. "What's wrong with you, Jake? Every time I see you lately, you're weirder than the time before. And don't tell me you're acting this way because I polished my nails!"

"You know what's weird?" I blurt. "It's weird that we got together because of Honor Society. Because I felt sorry for you. That's an odd way to start a relationship, isn't it? Feeling sorry for someone."

"You felt sorry for me?" Her eyes open wide; she looks wounded. I don't care.

"Sitting there, crying like that. How could I help it?"

"Are you saying you feel sorry for me now?"

"I'm saying it was a strange way to begin."

We've dropped our voices to fierce whispers, not wanting to disturb people at other tables. "You didn't have to call me!" she says.

A shadow looms above her head. I look up. The waitress with our steaks.

"Careful now, the platters are hot. You need any steak sauce?"

"No. We're fine."

By the time the waitress leaves, Callie's more composed and I'm ashamed of myself for being so mean to her. "That's why you didn't tell me about the headaches, isn't it?" she asks as she mashes butter into her baked potato. "Because you didn't want me to feel sorry for you."

For a second I'm lost. What headaches?

Being The Great Liar means never losing track.

"But I wouldn't have cared if you had a problem." She cuts into her steak, revealing red layers of meat beneath the seared crust. "I would have wanted to help you. If there's something wrong, I wish you'd just trust me."

"I do trust you," The Great Liar says.

Either way, it's not going to work. Lying to someone you care about, every minute of every day, would eat

111

away at us in no time. Judging from my lousy disposition, it already has.

And telling the truth? Forget it. Maybe Callie doesn't think so, but she'd be grossed out. And too nice to admit it. She'd feel honor-bound to pretend everything was the same. She'd stay with me out of pity until I became pitiful for real, and she'd resent me every minute we were together. I'd rather lose her now.

It's the first time I can remember eating a steak during wrestling season and having it taste like a piece of leather.

One of Life's Little Lessons.

But when we finish eating and the time comes to actually say something, to actually break up with her, I don't have the guts.

CHAPTER 15

We have practice all through the holidays, partly to keep on weight but mainly to get ready for the Midwinter Tournament at New Year's – the one where I was named Outstanding Wrestler last year. It's a big two-day meet three hours away in Redmond. We'll leave the day before weigh-ins and come back New Year's Eve. Lousy as Christmas has been, I'm looking forward to it.

Because now, in addition to everything else, The Great Liar has another secret to keep. The secret of Wanda Custer. Every day over the break, she shows up at practice. She's even taken the streaks out of her hair. No orange. No purple. Just short, straight brown hair that sits on her head like a cap.

Although she gives no outward hint, I know she's doing this because of the misguided pep talk I gave her that day we were waiting for rides in front of the gym. I never should have referred to her rainbow hair. I never should have told her the difference between her and Pole was that Pole works and she doesn't. All anybody wanted was for her to quit the team and leave us alone. Me included.

Now I've created a monster.

Twice more I've seen her at the Y, lifting. Both times I left before she could notice me. Once, driving home from the store, I saw her running along the street – running pretty fast. She's working her tail off. If she didn't have such a rotten disposition about it, I'd feel sorry for her.

At practice, she does the drills with this ferocious look on her face, like she's angry at everybody just for being there. She frowns all the time. She snarls, "Buzz off" to anybody who gives her grief. She slams her gear around. I'm not sure if this is an act or if she's really upset because she's putting in so much time and not improving much. I want to tell her that, Gender Equity or no, nobody gets strong overnight. And if you're a girl, you don't get as strong as a guy, period. Relax, Wanda.

But she doesn't. She stalks off the mat every time Pole pins her in about two seconds. Her jaw clenches with rage when our other lightweight does the same, a guy so small he actually weighs less than she does.

She's not taking any of this lightly.

So now we not only have Wanda Custer practicing with us every day; now we have Wanda Custer with an attitude.

The last thing I want anyone to know is that Wanda's newfound dedication is the result of my encouragement.

Other than that, things are looking up. Wanda might be wrestling badly, but I'm not. I'm hitting all my moves, feeling good, looking forward to Colby Douglas at the tournament. At home, things have calmed down, partly because Chopper's gotten his lenses and thinks he looks like a stud (no chance), even though he still reaches to push up his glasses every thirty seconds and is surprised each time he finds they're not there. As to Callie, I don't have to deal with her because the Maynard Singers are off on their holiday trip. For whatever reason, my mood brightens. The day we leave for Redmond, I'm ready. I'm psyched.

As usual, our motel is a dive, but that's not entirely

a negative. Coach doesn't take the whole team to tournaments, only the varsity, and since the rooms are cheap, I
luck out by having only Marcus for a roommate. I'm spared
Brian Fensel's stupid jokes. Spared Brunson's snoring.

We spend the evening working out in the Redmond
gym. Then we go for a run in the woods outside the motel.
It's about as warm as it ever gets this time of year, almost
balmy. The rotting leaves make a soft, springy path under
our feet, and send up a sweet, damp, mulchy smell that
makes me think of summer. Running's not usually my
favorite thing, but that night I don't mind it. My weight's
good. I'm ready.

Back in the room, Marcus sheds his sweats and then
takes forever untying his shoes, long enough to make sure I
notice them – a brand-new pair of expensive, high-tech
cross-trainers he must have gotten for Christmas. I watch
him fiddle with the laces but don't comment. There's nothing like being ignored to drive Marcus crazy.

He pulls off the shoes slowly, like someone per-
forming a sacred rite. Then, as if in slow-motion, he carries
them across the room and drops them in the trash can.

I can't bear to let this go. "You trying to make some
kind of statement?"

Having captured my attention, he grins. "You got a
problem with that?"

"I'm just hurt that you'd discard hundred-dollar
shoes without offering them to me first."

"Not your size, man."

I raise my eyebrows.

"A gift from the Coke-Man," he says – his name for
his mother's boyfriend. "Not given in the proper spirit of
the season, if you know what I mean."

"Ah." I nod, then shake my head. "Still seems like a shame not to profit off them some way. Bet you could sell them."

"Not in my neighborhood. My mother found out, she'd be pissed." He looks at the almost-new tread on the bottom of the shoes sticking out of the trash. "But if I lose them on an away trip, hey, that's different. You know how unfocused I am. Can't remember nothing. They sent me to the Alternative School all those times. I lose a pair of shoes on an away trip, everybody understands."

I know this is true, but it seems dumb. Typical Marcus, smart but dumb. "A very unfriendly gesture to your possible new Daddy," I say.

"He ain't never going to be my new Daddy." He scowls, drops onto the bed, searches for the TV remote. I shouldn't have made that crack about a new Daddy.

"Other than that, how was your Christmas?" I ask, trying to brighten up.

"Yeah, well you try spending Christmas in a project like Booker T, man. You know what you get?"

"What?"

"Either hundred-dollar shoes or nothing. Some kids get nothing." He gets up from the bed and moves the phone, checks out the night table, still looking for the remote.

"What about all those charities you see on TV?" I ask him. "What about that Angel Tree they have in the mall? I thought people gave gifts for kids over there."

"Yeah . . . like you're eight years old and some white dude buys you a shirt you wouldn't be caught dead in."

Marcus has a point. I want to say something neutral to calm him down, but he's in a mood now, so I keep quiet.

We search for the remote, pulling the covers off the bed, opening drawers. Marcus runs his hands along the top of the dresser like a blind man trying to find it by feel, shoving everything onto the floor, making a mess.

Then I spot it, fallen into the top of his open gear bag. I pick it up, hold it out to him. "Right under your nose."

Marcus gives a rough laugh, more like a snort. He channel surfs a while, then switches between a rerun of *In Living Color* and the movie on HBO. We're finished talking.

A bumpy evening. I escape by falling asleep.

Not until the next morning after weigh-ins, when Coach sends us to the McDonald's around the corner to get breakfast, do I realize I've forgotten my pills.

Not just forgotten to take them. Forgotten to bring them. They're sitting in the bathroom at home, three hours away.

This occurs to me as I wedge between Marcus and Brian Fensel and take a long sip of orange juice, which tastes like nectar for the gods after dehydrating all yesterday. At home, I always take my morning pills with orange juice.

"Christ!" I say without thinking.

"What?" Fensel talks through a mouthful of food.

"I forgot my allergy pills."

"You planning an allergy attack?"

"You never know."

Fensel resumes chewing.

I can't believe I'd be so stupid.

Couple of hours ago I was thinking how dumb Marcus is – and all the time I was ten times dumber.

Everybody turns their concentration back to their sausage biscuits or Egg McMuffins, pretty quiet as they concentrate on stuffing their mouths. I remember Dr. Symmes saying you should never stop your medicine all at once. I calculate that I haven't had a pill for over twenty-four hours, since the night before last.

Is that possible?

Not only possible, but true. Now that I think of it, I forgot the pills yesterday morning, too, in the commotion of getting ready for the trip.

But hey— This is not the first time I've failed to take them. Mom would have a fit if she knew this, but every once in a while I forget and so far it's no big deal. I take the next pill and carry on. No sweat.

Okay, so this time I've missed a couple of doses, a day and a half. But nothing's happened. I remember Dad saying my whole diagnosis might be a fluke. Maybe he's right. Maybe it was the flu. Or hitting my head. Or some other kind of weirdness. I might be cured. Sure I might. Why not?

This is as good a time as any to test the theory.

Not that I have much choice.

Also, here's the critical thing: I have to concentrate on wrestling. Not on pills. Not on some disaster that might happen but probably won't. The worst thing I can do is let myself be distracted. What I came here for is to wrestle. That's what I decide.

Back in the gym, I start warming up right away. They're wrestling three mats and it's going fast. You'd think with all my determination it would be easier than usual, but it isn't. I get the jitters like always, all the spit in my mouth dries up, I feel like I'm never going to break a sweat. There are a lot of teams here, and I see guys from all over the state, guys I've beat and guys who beat me in the days before I knew what I was doing.

I don't spot Colby until they call his name to wrestle, right before my own first match. He has to walk past me on his way to check in with the scorekeepers. When our eyes meet, it's like looking into a mirror. I can tell he notices it, too. We're the same height, same build, both with light brown hair, blue eyes, tawny skin. Last year at regionals, Brian made some crack about our looking like twins, but I didn't notice it then. Now the only difference I see is that his face is narrower than mine and his nose a little longer.

"How you doing?" we both say at the same time.

My voice is deeper than his.

Otherwise, it's eerie.

Then I watch him wrestle, and I'm reminded how different we are, after all. My signature is a low single; his is riding legs. Before first period is over, he has his opponent tied up in a braid, legs around the other guy's so tight he can't wriggle out, can't get up, can't do anything.

"The only way you can defend against legs," Coach's voice says from over my shoulder, "is to stay on your feet. Because once you let him get his legs in, it's like having a boa constrictor on you."

"I remember," I say, recalling regionals last year, right at the end, when Colby was about to beat me.

Coach slaps me on the back. "You're better this year," he says before he moves away.

Sweat pours from me like water. The whole time I've been watching Colby, I've also been jogging in place. This sweat is a very good sign.

I beat my first guy in the first period. There are six-teen teams at the meet, so I only have to wrestle once more to get to the semis, which start the next morning. Colby makes the semis, too. All day I watch him. He's good. But so am I. Coach is right. I *am* better this year. Smoother. Faster. Better at staying on my feet. When I face Colby tomorrow, I'll give him his best match this season. I have a good chance to win. By the time we leave the gym at the end of that first day, I have visions of doing a repeat performance as Outstanding Wrestler of the Redmond Midwinter Tournament.

For a guy who gets so nervous he can hardly break a sweat, this is big thinking. For the first time since break-fast I remember I don't have my pills. It doesn't matter. I'm okay. I'm going to get away with it.

This is the exact thought that comes to me: *I'm going to get away with it.*

It's still warm outside. It's been drizzling all day, and now such a thick fog hangs in the air that it feels like we're walking through clouds. Later, when we run in the damp woods behind our motel, the water beads on our skin but doesn't make us cold. A strong scent rises from the rot-ting leaves, sweet and musky at the same time. It's as if we can smell each individual leaf decaying under our feet. It's pleasant for a while, then gets overpowering. Cheesy and rank. Almost sickening. It comes and goes even back in the room, even after I shower. Stays with me all night while I sleep.

Next thing I know, Marcus rolls over and pokes at me. "Time to get up, man."

"Huh?"

"Didn't you hear the alarm?"

I guess I did, but I'm not ready. The nasty smell is back. I don't open my eyes.

"No kidding, Jake. Move. Coach wants us out there by seven."

"It's not even light," I mumble.

"It's the middle of the winter, moron."

I hear him roll out of bed, go into the bathroom. I don't open my eyes. Finally, still bleary, I make myself sit. Marcus has turned on the light over by the sink, but the room is dark. I can't make myself wake up.

Reaching over to the night table, I feel around for the remote. Nothing. I turn my head to the right, toward the night table, to see if I can spot it in the dim light.

But my head doesn't point where I aim it. Something pulls at my neck, makes me look to the left at the curtain against the window.

What the hell?

I fight against it. Try to jerk my head in the proper direction. It won't move. Won't move anywhere.

Panic slices through me. My mouth fills with saliva. Huge amounts, all the spit that isn't there when I get nervous before a match. I need to swallow.

I can't. The muscles in my neck are frozen.

I'm going to choke on my own spit.

My heart beats about a million times a second.

I'm going to drown.

Then I feel myself falling. Since I'm sitting on the bed, I know there isn't far to go. I also know Marcus isn't in the bed anymore, but it's as if someone is there beside me – someone I know is imaginary even as I give him this mental warning: *Get out of the way, man, I'm coming over.*

That's all I remember before I black out. Speaking to that imaginary guy.

CHAPTER 16

Marcus is looming over me when I open my eyes. Standing over the bed, looking down like Chopper did the other times, a different face but with the identical expression of terror.

"Oh, shit," I mumble.

"You can say that again."

Although I'm not quite connected yet, I register his voice clearly, like a patch of sun seeping through the clouds. Register the fearful tone. Register the fact that the bad smell is gone.

Otherwise, my head is all fog. I feel like I've walked a thousand miles across rough terrain. I want to sleep.

"Jesus, man," Marcus says as I struggle to keep my eyes open. He fingers his lucky earring like it's a charm that will save us. "I thought you was gone."

"Wishful thinking," I hear my voice say.

I'm watching the scene from a long way off. I'm in the picture, but separated from it, too. Like dreaming, but knowing I'm not. Wake up, I tell myself. Stay awake.

Then the clouds.

Then Coach.

Beads of sweat on his forehead, a high, white domed curve.

"Epilepsy," he says, the word floating around us, all its jagged edges. He's talking to Marcus. Explaining.

How does he know?

Coming back is slow, like lifting a foot out of quicksand.

"You're all right," he says.

I guess I am. I try to sit.

"You can sleep a while," he adds, worried-sounding.

I do sit. *Epilepsy.* Creepy word.

"How did you know?" I ask.

"How do you feel?" He paces back and forth, eyes never leaving my face.

"I'm okay." No upset stomach like the last time. Just tired. And the fog. I shake my head to clear it.

"How did you know?" I ask again.

"Your mother," he says.

Of course.

To Marcus he says, "The worst thing that can happen is what you just saw. That's it, that's the end of it. It's not dangerous unless he hurts himself falling."

"Yeah, well he did all right. Fell right on the bed." Marcus turns to me. "You shoulda told me, man."

"Didn't tell anybody." I sound like a little kid. "Don't *you* tell, either." Begging.

Coach puts his hand on Marcus's shoulder. "This goes no farther than this room." As if he speaks for both of them.

The wisps clear, one by one. I come out of the fog enough to know that Marcus likes attention too much to keep a secret. From now on, everyone will know.

Everyone.

And then this: the memory of my neck turning. Muscles paralyzed, unable to swallow.

This was not something people told me about afterwards.

I was there.

Until now, I never quite believed it.

Sorry, Dad. No chance freak week is over.

Even if it only happened because I forgot the medicine, it's too late.

This really happened.

This is real.

The fog is gone. My mind is clear.

My mood is black.

• • •

Coach sends Marcus off with the team. When we're alone, he goes to the window, pulls the curtain open a little, looks out.

"We'll say you got sick," he tells me. "I called your folks. They're on their way."

For the moment, I don't register what this means.

Coach drops into the chair by the window. He digs a toothpick from his pocket and chews on it for a while.

"Did you think if you told me I'd kick you off the team?" he asks finally. "My number one wrestler?"

"You knew anyway. Without my telling you." I imagine the long, deep conversation he must have had with Mom.

"I would have admired you more if you told me yourself."

A slant of early sun comes through the opened curtain. I see that the covers are knocked off the bed, the sheets pulled free.

"Even if I wanted to kick you off the team, I couldn't. Any more than I could kick Wanda off."

"Gender Equity and Handicap Equity, too." I picture my neck turning in the wrong direction like something out of *The Exorcist*. Under some other, evil kind of control.

Coach throws the toothpick away.

"Look at me, Jake."

I do, but I'm seeing a freak with his head pulled to the left, choking on his own saliva, falling over on an imaginary companion who wasn't there.

It was better when I didn't know. At least then I had hope.

"When you have a goal and the talent and will to achieve it – that's about as good as it gets," Coach says. "Take it from a man who's been around long enough to know."

I wonder what kind of noise I made, to bring Marcus running out of the bathroom.

"Everybody has problems. You work around them. You keep going."

I wonder how much time passed. Wonder when Marcus called Coach.

"You hear me? You keep going."

This gets my attention. Coach was two-time state champion in high school and wrestled varsity in college until he broke his leg skiing and never came back. "You mean keep going until you slam into the wall that stops you?"

He ignores my sarcasm. "Exactly. Keep going until you can't."

I picture myself writhing on the bed. I wonder how long Marcus had to look at it.

Coach frowns, brings his eyebrows together, a carroty bush. "Pay attention, Jake."

"I am."

"Where's your medicine?"

I shrug.

"What's that mean?" He shrugs back, a parody.

"At home. I forgot it." Too tired to be clever, too slow to be The Great Liar.

"You forgot?"

"I'm all right, Coach. Once it happens, it's over. You're a little sleepy for a while, but then you're fine."

"There's such a thing as filling a prescription out of town. If you forget your pills, you can replace them. All it takes is a phone call. We're not on the moon."

"It was stupid, but I'm okay." The black mood lightens a notch as I realize this seizure ended like my first one, when I woke up afterwards and felt fine. "Like you said, it's not a problem that stops you. I'm okay. I can wrestle."

"Not today, you can't."

I stare at him. His expression is stony.

"If you're not going to take care of yourself, who will? You're a senior, Jake. You're a team captain. This was irresponsible. What if you were diabetic and forgot your insulin?"

"This is different."

"It's the same." There is no warmth in his voice, no sympathy.

"Come on, Coach."

"Nobody faults you for having a seizure. If it happened because you didn't take your medicine, that's another story. Then it *is* your fault."

"Coach, I'm sorry."

"Coach Wallace will stay here till your parents come. It'll be a couple of hours."

"I don't need a babysitter."

"You have time for a nap."

"I'm not sleepy."

He gets up, expressionless now. "Then get dressed. Watch TV. Read a good book." He spots my bag on the floor, its contents spilling out. He reaches in and throws me a shirt.

"I'll see you next week at practice."

I sit there after he goes, my mind entirely clear now, not that this will do me any good. I am not going to wrestle Colby Douglas. Not going to be Outstanding Wrestler.

I am not going to get away with anything.

• • •

They both show up. Dad at the wheel, Mom tight-lipped and worried.

"The medicine is not something you can ignore," she says as we drive off. "It's not optional. If you've learned that, this will be worth it."

Right.

Dad says, "The doctor said this could happen if you withdraw the pills. It could happen to anybody."

"Not to somebody without epilepsy," I say.

"You don't know."

I do.

If I could name what despair feels like, running through my veins the way it does all the way home, I would say, sour milk, cow manure, turkey dung, maybe a combination of all three. I stretch out on the back seat and sleep heavy the whole three hours, rottenness coursing through me like bad dreams.

When we get home, Mom tells me not even to think

about driving. For at least a month. "This is no joke, Jake. I catch you driving, I'll report you to the DMV."

As if I were a criminal on parole, bound to lapse.

The next day she arranges for me to see Dr. Symmes, even though it's New Year's Eve and everything else in the world is closed. Dr. Symmes is smart enough to see me alone. We leave Mom in the waiting room.

"This isn't unusual," she says after writing down what happened. "Even the fact that the seizure came on after you were halfway awake. The only danger would be if the seizure didn't limit itself to a couple of minutes. If it kept on and on. We see that sometimes. You were fortunate."

"Fortunate. Right."

"The neurons in your brain are always firing, sending your body messages to move or talk or whatever. What the medication does is slow your brain down just enough that they can't start firing wildly and make you jerk like they do in a seizure." She draws her brows together, and her face gathers itself into a maze of worried wrinkles. "Sometimes when the medication is withdrawn too quickly, the neurons start that rapid firing and it's hard to stop it. In your case, that didn't happen."

"So this is from forgetting the medicine? It wouldn't have happened anyway?"

"My personal guess is, it's from not taking the medicine." She takes off her half-glasses and sets them down on my chart. "But officially – who knows?"

"So you don't have a clue," I say.

"A lot of people, no matter what we do, we never get their seizures quite under control. If I were you, Jake, I'd assume it was from forgetting the pills and get religious about taking them. If I were you, I'd consider myself lucky."

I stand up and thank her. I never thought I'd be so sick of hearing that I'm lucky.

• • •

"Callie's back in town," Chopper informs me when I get home. He peers through no-longer-spectacled eyes, which for some reason make him look older. "She called and wants you to call her back." He pauses. "You going to tell her?"

"About my major setback, you mean?"

"About your problem in general."

"What makes you think she doesn't know already?"

"Brains." He taps his head. "The genetic material that skipped the older brother."

"Don't you wish."

"You just don't have the nerve." He cocks his head, daring me to argue with him. The contact lenses have made him brave. "Well? You going to tell her?"

I shrug, but the answer is no. By now the whole team is probably talking about it. It's New Year's Eve. They'll all be out tonight, running their mouths. She'll know soon enough.

Which doesn't mean Chopper hasn't hit on something. I don't have the nerve. I'm not about to tell her anything. To risk becoming her object of pity. Not now, not later, not ever. No way.

But there's one thing I can do before she hears the news and feels she has to stay with me out of duty.

I can set her free.

CHAPTER 17

Coward that I am, my first thought is to break up with her over the phone. I dial her number. She answers on the first ring.

"Jake!" Her breathy voice makes my heart pick up its pace. Not what I expected. "How'd you do at the tournament?"

"Fine," The Great Liar says. "How'd you do at competition?"

"Second! Can you believe it? Fifty choruses from all over the country and we got second!"

"That's great. Great."

"It was. I'll tell you about it tonight."

"Listen, about tonight—"

"What?"

"I can't use the car."

"But it's New Year's Eve!" Her voice rises with impatience. Then she sighs. "Maybe I can get Mom's car."

"No. I mean—" This is not how I planned to begin. "It's a long story."

"Oh, Jake. You're not grounded again, are you? Not after we haven't seen each other all this time."

"Listen, Callie—"

"I am listening."

"It's not just the car. It's—"

"What?"

"I'm not sure I can go at all."

"You can't go out?"

"It's not a matter of can't. It's more—"

"Are you saying you don't want to?" Softer now, a little catch in her voice.

"It's not—"

"Just tell me, Jake. Do you want to go out with me or not?"

"No."

A long silence.

"I don't believe you," she finally says.

This is not what The Great Liar expects.

I take a breath, regroup. "Listen, Callie, when we got back from the tournament I realized— I realized—" I'm not sure what words ought to follow, and none do. We end up listening to each other breathe into the phone like perverts.

"Listen, Jake," she says after a while, crisp and determined. "I don't know what's wrong with you, but discussing it over the phone doesn't get it. I'm going to ask my mother for the car. I'll pick you up at nine-thirty. Period, no talkbacks."

And she hangs up.

• • •

The New Year's party is at Steven Wills' house, where everyone is going because his parents are out of town. I'm not sure I can face it. But when Callie shows up, it's clear she means us to go. She's all in black: black skirt, black sweater, black hair pulled back from her face, hanging loose around her shoulders, red lipstick that shows off her white-white skin. Big silver hoops in her ears. She looks terrific.

Steven lives only four blocks away. It takes two minutes to get there. On the way Callie pretends our telephone conversation never happened.

"About before—" I start.

She reaches over, puts her finger to my lips. She's wearing some kind of spicy perfume. "Save it. We haven't seen each other for a while. We have all night. Maybe it will go away."

This will never go away, I think. But I save it.

At Steven's, the crowd overflows from his basement upstairs into the kitchen. There's our usual group and a few surprises, like Zane Dennis, the druggie, who sometimes shows up at these things because he lives nearby. But no wrestlers. Nothing about the tournament was in the paper today, so it must have ended too late for Coach to call in the results. They probably got back into town about two or three this morning. Just time to rest up for New Year's Eve. Not that most of them travel in my social circle. But still. At best I'll be saved from public humiliation another few hours.

Music blares up from the basement, so loud the rhythm makes a drumbeat in my throat. Steven's parents know some of his friends are coming over. I bet they have no clue how many. They've filled coolers of soda, made Steven promise not to allow any alcohol. All the same, the beer flows. Some guy I don't know offers us one. Callie says no. She doesn't drink, doesn't smoke, never has. Usually I don't drink during the season, and not much any time, but after the last couple of days, and considering the conversation I'm about to have with Callie, I accept.

We go downstairs, get caught up in the crowd. The music is wild. People shout over the noise but can't really hear each other. At least no one is going to ask how I did at the tournament. Not that they care. Callie squeezes my hand. We dance. Already I feel the beer in my fingers and my feet. Between songs, someone hands me another. I drink it too fast. The buzz smoothes out all my rough edges. I forget my mission.

Just before twelve, someone turns off the music and switches on the TV. Everyone turns to watch the ball drop in Times Square. We herald the New Year with noisemakers and paper streamers flying across the room, landing in our hair. Callie and I kiss for a long time. When the music starts again, slow and dreamy, we move together to the rhythm, but we keep kissing.

"What was it you wanted to tell me?" she whispers when we pause to take a breath.

I pull her closer. "Not now."

"I knew it would go away when we saw each other."

"It didn't go away, but it can wait." My head is filled with the scented silk of Callie's hair. Out of the corner of my eye I spot Brunson, our heavyweight. First wrestler of the evening. If anyone knows the truth, Brunson does. I'm drunk enough not to care.

Callie stops dancing. "If your problem with me didn't go away, then it can't wait, either." She takes my hand and leads me out of the crowd, up the steps, through the kitchen and into the empty den. "Now," she tells me.

She's right. Now. But all I do is stand there.

"Tell me, Jake."

I'm not sure I can. I arrange myself on the edge of a wingback chair. Take my time. "It's just that when I got back from the tournament yesterday I realized— I realized that while you were gone, I—"

"Jake, just tell me!"

"I enjoyed the freedom," I blurt. "Not because of you . . . Because . . ."

Callie crosses her arms in front of her as if to protect herself. "Because of what?"

"Because I feel like we're tying each other down. Because if it's going to be a new year, both of us deserve to start it . . . " This is sounding worse and worse. "I'm not saying this the way I mean to, Callie."

"You're saying all that kissing was just an act."

"I'm not saying that at all. This is nothing personal."

"Nothing personal!" She tosses her hair.

"It's not because of you, it's because of me. If you knew—" Which she will, probably before the end of the night.

"Knew what?"

"It's not what you think. It's no reflection on you. It's not a personal thing."

"I see." She hugs herself as if she's cold. "It's so impersonal you didn't even want to tell me in person."

I want to put my arms around her, make her warm. This is cruel.

I remind myself not letting her go would be worse.

"You're right," I say. "I didn't want to do this in person. It would have been easier on the phone."

Next thing I know, she's gone. Grabbed her coat and stomped out of the house. That quick.

The room feels about twenty degrees colder.

• • •

"Girlfriend dump you?" Zane Dennis, beer in one hand, cigarette in the other, is standing in the kitchen when

I come out of the den, looking sly, almost smiling.

"I guess your loser druggie buddies decided they were too good to bring in the New Year with you," I say.

He blows a perfect smoke ring, then puts down his beer long enough to lift his hand, touch his index and middle fingers together to show closeness. "Steven and I are like this."

"Right." I open the refrigerator and take a beer from someone's six-pack, I don't know whose.

"Got something that'll cure your blues better than that," Zane says.

"I bet you do." I pop the top, take a long swallow. Zane reaches into a pocket, brings out his usual plastic baggie – not full of pills this time but of white powder. For all I know, it's a packet of cornstarch.

"Get lost, Zane."

"Beer's a downer," he says. "You're already down. I can tell, man. What you need is this." He shakes the baggie at my face. Since the last time I saw him, his hair has grown. It's blond, greasy, pulled back into a slimy pony tail. It occurs to me that if I strangle him, I'll be doing the world a service.

"Come on, man," he says, beckoning me toward the hallway.

I open the refrigerator and grab a second beer. "Got all the help I need, man," I say, holding up the two cans. Zane shrugs and disappears into the bathroom down the hall. I pop open the second beer, sip from one and then the other. Tommy LaCosta stumbles up the stairs from the basement, heads for the bathroom.

"Occupied," I say.

He pounds on the door and shouts, "Hurry up!"

When Zane comes out, he's transformed. Eyes darting in every direction, face glossy with sweat. Tommy lurches into the bathroom. Zane grins.

"You're missing the best twenty minutes of your life," he tells me.

"I'll pass," I say. This is scientific. My medicine slows down my brain just enough so it won't fire wildly. The last thing I want is to speed it up and spazz out, especially in front of half the population of Maynard High School. No speed. No coke. No crack. No, sir. But alcohol, that's a different story. Alcohol slows you down. Blots you out. Keeps you mellow.

I carry both my beers back downstairs into the noise. The room's so thick and smoky no one notices Callie's not with me. I find a couch, sit down, take a drink. The music is deafening, which seems just right. A girl sits next to me, shouts into my ear that her name is Jenny or Penny, I can't tell which. She starts laughing. She leans against me. I let her.

My blood is getting carbonated, not in a pleasant way. Chopper once researched a paper about how some people are born with a tendency toward alcoholism and some aren't. I think I'm one of the aren'ts. But I keep drinking. Jenny or Penny nestles her head against my shoulder. Everything's buzzing. Buzzing but not quite numb.

For weeks breaking up with Callie has been in the back of my mind. Now it's done, the pressure's off. Ten minutes ago – and already here's Jenny or Penny, willing to take her place.

So why do I feel so rotten?

• • •

I lose track of time. I'm dancing. People are looking at me. My friend Steven says, "That's enough, Jake. Don't put on a show."

You haven't seen anything, pal, I think. *Wait till you hear about the performance I can do late at night or early in the morning.*

Just wait.

Next thing I remember, I'm outside in air so cold that I know I've forgotten my jacket. Steven's house is behind me, dark and empty. I'm staggering. Where's my car? If I'm drunk, who's the designated driver? A thin sliver of fear punches through me. The last thing I need is a DWI.

Then I remember: I can't drive for a month.

My stomach turns over. I'm reeling, retching, sick. I stumble toward the bushes beside Steven's house and puke until I'm empty and dry.

"Hey, man." A familiar voice, but for a second I can't place it. I squint into the darkness. Brunson. "Rough break, getting sick at the tournament," he says.

"Mmmnh," I mumble. What's he mean, "getting sick at the tournament"?

His strong arms help me up. I'm too weak to shrug him off. He leads me to his car, drives me home. Nothing I can do about it, so I let him.

"Thanks, man." I stumble into the house and drop into bed.

Sometime the next afternoon, I start the year the way millions of other people do, with a headache big as the world.

Getting up takes all my will power. I move slowly so as not to jiggle my head while I pull on a pair of sweats, shuffle to the kitchen, swig orange juice and aspirin. Mom eyes me with suspicion. I don't think I can keep down my pills, but I take them for her benefit. Dad's in the den watching football. Chopper follows me back to my room.

"What the hell's wrong with you?" He pulls the door shut. "Don't you know getting drunk makes it easier for you to have a seizure?" he spits in a furious whisper.

"Relax, cyber-man. You've got it backwards. When you have a seizure, your brain speeds up. Alcohol slows you down."

"You're the one who's got it wrong. Alcohol lowers the threshold for having a seizure. Makes it easier, not harder. What are you trying to do, kill yourself?"

"Take a good look, Chopper. Nobody here is having a seizure, only a hangover."

"Yeah, because this time you were lucky." His face is white with fury. When he turns away, he crashes his hand into the door to slam it, then catches it at the last second, closes it without a sound.

Chopper cares about me more than I do myself.

Too nauseated to move, I flop on the bed and drift in and out of sleep, half-listening for the phone to ring. For it to be Callie.

It doesn't happen.

For supper, Mom sets out sandwiches. I choke one down, then leave the table to throw up again. Someone's left the sports page open on the bathroom floor. There's a small headline: *Maynard Seniors Score in Midwinter Tourney.* When I finish heaving, I read the article. Marcus won his weight class, which he'd hoped he would since Lizard Smith wasn't at the tournament and Marcus thought he could wrestle at least even with everybody else. Fensel got fourth at 160, and Brunson came in second for the heavyweights. It occurs to me that I never asked Brunson about this while he was driving me home. Award for Outstanding Wrestler went to 145-pounder, Colby Douglas.

When I stand up and catch sight of my pale face in the mirror, I look more like Zane Dennis than I look like myself.

Is this what you want, buddy? I think.

Hell, yes. For a whole day I've been too sick to worry about starting school tomorrow, when everybody will know the truth: that Jake Chapman is not a superstar after all, but a freak who passes out from time to time and has convulsions in his bed.

CHAPTER 18

The next day at school, I make an effort not to catch anybody's eye in the hallways. Not to notice whatever expressions of curiosity and pity might be on their faces. You're not supposed to leave the grounds at lunch time, but I do. Otherwise I might run into Callie in the cafeteria. I throw away my sandwich, pull on a sweatshirt, and run downtown as far as the river. It's a nice day and there are lots of joggers, so nobody notices me. I get back just in time for calculus. By the end of the day my stomach's growling, but my head is perfectly clear. I've gotten through a whole day of school without talking to anybody except teachers.

If I can keep this up till graduation, I'm set.

I have no intention of going to practice.

While I'm at my locker, packing my books to go home, Marcus taps me on the shoulder.

"You all right, man?"

"Yeah, fine." I slam the locker shut.

"Figured you would be."

"Yeah. Well." I hike my backpack to my shoulder, make for the door.

"Wrestling room's the other way, man," he says, keeping pace with me.

"I know where the wrestling room is."

"Figured you'd wuss out," he tells me.

"You did, huh?"

"Yeah. Your record is good, but you know—Always a wimp underneath." He's grinning. I'm not. I stop and face him. He's wearing his most earnest expression.

"I didn't tell nobody," he says.

"*That* would be a miracle."

"I didn't, man. Come on." He turns in the direction of the wrestling room. Though I'm not sure I believe him, I feel I have no choice but to follow him to practice.

• • •

It's true: Nobody's looking at me funny, nobody asks how I feel except Pole who wants to know if my allergies are better and is satisfied when I say, "Much." Marcus hasn't told. Startling as this is, I know it's not forever. Marcus doesn't have it in him to keep it up.

Coach pretends nothing has happened, so I do, too. There's never going to be a minute from now on when I'm not waiting for Marcus to spill his guts, but for the time being I practice hard, focus, try to forget. I'm too wired to want to go home when we get finished. Mom's out of town again, Dad's working evenings, Chopper's probably browsing the Web. I think about changing into my street clothes and trying to bum a ride home, but in the end I don't. Instead I run the mile from school to the Y and lift weights. Then I run the two miles home. This after running at lunch, too. I was glad not to have to face Callie in the cafeteria, but now it occurs to me she must have changed her route between classes to keep from seeing me in the hallways. I'm not the only one shirking contact. I'd be more disturbed except that by the time I get home I can hardly keep my eyes open.

Exhaustion, I decide, numbs your brain just as well as beer.

I like it so much that I follow the same schedule of running and lifting all week, except the one night we go out of town to a match. I work out Saturday and Sunday, too. Each day, I stress different muscles, follow the rule of not working the same muscle group more than every forty-eight hours. Truth is, if you lift weights every day, you have to be creative. I make up a routine I call the arm circuit, where I do one set of curls with dumbbells, then a set of overhead triceps, then curls with a curl bar, then different triceps, then curls with the straight bar, till my arms are about to fall off. I even start doing squats, which I usually don't include because Coach thinks they make wrestlers slow.

"What you need is upper body strength and quickness," Coach always says. "It doesn't matter how much you can squat if the guy has already shot in on you and is shoving your face into the mat."

I do squats anyway.

Toward the end of the week, Wanda Custer shows up in the weight room, which surprises me since she must be as exhausted as I am, the way she works like a demon at practice and spends the rest of her energy crabbing about not being able to compete with the guys. Although I'm not happy to see her, I'm finished avoiding her. You can avoid only so many people at one time. Wanda has the decency to leave me alone. She looks in my direction only when I'm doing bench presses, and I can't blame her because everybody else watches then, too.

In the last four years I've gained thirty-five pounds and my bench has gained about a hundred and seventy, which means the only high school guys who bench more than I do now are the beefer football linemen who outweigh me by more than a hundred pounds. I put everyone else around my weight to shame. So although Wanda is a nuisance, if she wants to watch, let her.

• • •

"You lifted again?" Chopper asks when I get home.
"A little."
"You go a lot."
"Astute observation."
"Next time take me with you," he says.
"Why? You thinking of taking up wrestling?"
"Are you kidding? You think I want to be you?"
We both consider this. Who would want to be me right now? Nobody. "Good point, Chopper.".
"I didn't mean it that way," he says. "I'm serious, Jake. You could teach me."
"Just what I need. A student."
"Who researched your term paper last semester?"
"You forget. I'm not allowed to drive. How will you get to the Y?"
"I'll find a way. I'll meet you."
He does.
Right away Chopper can bench a hundred pounds. For a skinny fourteen-year-old, not bad. But he can't do pull-ups worth diddley.
"That's pathetic," I tell him.
"What do you mean, pathetic? I can do the first one real easy. It just gets hard around two."
I roll my eyes. "Keep trying. You gotta get it started if you wanna get it done." This comes out sounding like a bad football-coach imitation, but Chopper eats it up.

• • •

After that, Chopper is dedicated. Wanda seems dedicated, too. The guys in the weight room don't like having her around, but I sense they admire her persistence. One night Wanda goes through her routine with the dumbbells, then lies down on the bench press and lifts a couple of the lightest plates. There's nobody there to spot her, and she's airplaning like crazy. That is, she's lifting faster with her left hand than her right, like most right-handed people do. For some reason, your stronger arm goes up slower, makes the bar slant, a little like a plane tipping its wings. I don't want to be bothered with this, but I have visions of Wanda dropping the bar on herself, so I go over and spot her.

"I did the same thing when I first started lifting," I tell her. "Coach told me to put five pounds extra on the fast side, and I did. It's a mental thing. I never airplaned again."

Wanda scowls. "Thanks Jake, but I didn't ask for advice." She sets down the bar, wriggles off the bench, huffs off.

Next time we're in the weight room, she puts extra weight on the left side, exactly like I told her, before she tries to bench.

From across the room, Chopper grins at me smugly. I feel like a babysitter.

• • •

We're into the main part of the season that counts against our conference record. I'm winning all my matches, but as Coach says, if you're a senior and a two-time state qualifier, you ought to. He also says our conference doesn't have anybody near as good as I am at 145, so I won't see my best competition until Colby Douglas at regionals.

So why do I feel slightly off my game? One night I'm wrestling against a guy who's not very strong, and I stupidly reach back for his head. "Never reach back," Coach has told us about a thousand times. I've heard it so much and done it by mistake so many times that by now I know by instinct it's wrong. But I know I can get away with it with this guy, and I do.

Afterwards, Coach is furious. "That nonsense might work with fish," he says, "but doing it the right way will work, too. The only difference is, doing it properly will also work against a good guy, while if you're lazy you'll end up on your back counting the lights. You've got to do it right *every time.*"

"I know." I can hardly look at him. Uncertainty is taking its toll. Any day now, Marcus will open his mouth. Any day now, I'll run into Callie. The sledge hammer that's hanging over my head is held aloft by the merest string.

But when I finally do see Callie – first time since New Year's – it's not what I expect. We have an away match, and I'm on my way from my locker to the activity bus when I spot Callie at the other end of the hall, heading straight toward me. She's walking so fast, at first I think she's coming over to talk. But when she spots me she turns her eyes down to the floor and passes right by. For a second I feel like a branding iron has been applied just below my ribs. Then I think: well, this isn't so bad. On the bus, I fall sound asleep, don't even listen to Brian Fensel's jokes. Don't give Callie another thought until the second period of my match.

I'm up against a guy who knows what he's doing, and though my wrestling isn't sterling, I'm doing okay.

Then I get a re-run of Callie's hair bouncing on her neck as she pretended not to see me. I lose my focus. He takes me down. In the end it doesn't make a difference; I recover and win. But it's scary. Next day, I run to the Y after practice and max out on the bench. We're almost finished the regular wrestling season, and I'm lifting more than I usually do at this point in the year, as much as I did at the beginning.

This ought to make me feel better, but instead I find myself wondering what good it does to have muscles if it doesn't stop you from throwing fits or from having to break up with your girlfriend in such a way that she's not even willing to look you in the eye.

• • •

"Do I look studly or what?" Chopper asks when Mom comes home for the weekend.

"Pretty studly," she says, and winks at me. He flexes a bicep and raises a muscle about the size of a grape. He casts a glance of admiration at his arm. The shirt he's wearing features a skull clasping a dagger in its mouth, and a caption that reads, *Mess with the Best, Die like the Rest.* Chopper strips off the shirt and flexes again.

"My chest is getting bigger already, don't you think so?" he asks Mom. His chest is winter-white and puny.

"You're filling out," Mom agrees. She's leafing through the week's mail, not really paying attention. Chopper doesn't care. He struts around the kitchen, furiously trying to raise the outline of his nonexistent pecs. Lately he lavishes the same attention on his body that he used to reserve for his computer.

"This is the first time you've seen me without my shirt on," he tells Mom. "That's why you're so awestruck."

"Stunned," Mom agrees as she studies the electric bill.

"I wouldn't sign up for Mr. America just yet," I tell him.

"You're jealous," he retorts.

He's joking, but in a way, he's right. He doesn't have any muscles yet, but if he keeps at it, he will. His body is responding to weight training exactly the way it's supposed to. His body is something he can count on, along with a brain that never deserts him in the no-man's-land between being asleep and being awake.

I remember the feeling.

Jealous? You bet.

• • •

"I hear you've been lifting every day," Coach tells me at practice. He doesn't look pleased. It's interesting how Coach hears almost everything.

"At some point, it's counterproductive," he tells me. "You get strong, but it costs you flexibility."

I shrug.

"Are you working on anything besides your bench?"

"Sure. I'm working on everything."

"But you're benching a lot. Maybe more than you should." He pauses to let that sink in. "I've been there, I know. It's seductive. People watch you and admire how much you can lift. It's flattering."

"I'm not Marcus. I'm not out for that kind of attention."

"The bench press is in the middle of the weight room. You're strong for your size. You can't help playing to the audience."

"But Coach—"

He holds up a hand to stop me. "You know what I think? I think you're working too hard. Lifting too much. Running too far. The day before a match, you ought to be coming in a couple of pounds up from your wrestling weight, not a couple of pounds under. I think you're wearing yourself out."

I shrug, but I don't care. I'm not planning to stop. I need the exercise. I need to be numb. If I weren't, all I'd feel was rage.

There's no explaining this, so I don't try.

CHAPTER 19

A couple of nights later I get home and find Chopper in the den with tall gangly girl named Margie who's started hanging around our house. She's the first girl he's ever brought over – I mean *ever* – and the fact that they're supposedly working on a computer-generated biology project doesn't fool me. On this particular night they're so intent they don't even hear me come in. With Mom at a meeting and Dad at work, the house feels emptier than usual – or maybe it's just the project I have in mind that sours my mood. I go upstairs and sit in front of the computer. There's something I need to do that's been nagging at me for weeks. I stare at the blank screen a long time.

Then I write my letter to the Navy.

I say how honored I feel to have been awarded a four-year ROTC scholarship. How sorry I am to turn it down. How, after thinking it over, I realize the military is not for me.

By the time I print out the letter and sign it, the muscles in my throat are so tight I can barely swallow.

I shower, but it doesn't relax me. This is not one of the nights when numbness helps.

Downstairs, Chopper and Margie are still deep in conversation.

"Alta Vista," Margie whispers.

Chopper shakes his head. "Yahoo."

Margie giggles. "No way! I like Excite."

If you didn't know better, you'd think they were try-ing out slightly off-color pet names. But this isn't love-talk, it's an ongoing discussion about the search engines on the Web. They can't agree which ones are best. For some rea-son, it comforts me that Chopper's fascinated more by Margie's interest in cyberspace than by her feminine appeal.

They look in my direction and register shock. "I didn't know you were home," Chopper says.

"Got here an hour ago," I tell him. I make myself address an envelope, find a stamp, and mail my letter.

• • •

Half the wrestling team is out with a stomach virus. Coach is upset. Our next regular-season match against Riverside is coming up, and ever since Marcus made us lose to them by grabbing his crotch, Coach has been keyed up for a big comeback. By the day of the meet, we're still miss-ing four varsity guys, including Marcus and Brunson. As for me, I don't have the virus, but my shoulder's sore from too much weight-lifting, just as Coach predicted. Although it's not serious, Coach glares at me every time he spots the ice pack the trainer gave me.

When Riverside's team shows up, it's clear they're not going to face us with dignity and grace. Instead, they've brought along a little surprise designed to mess with our minds. They've brought their scale. Big as life, strapped to a seat at the back of their activity bus.

For the uninitiated, this is not some little bathroom-type scale; this is the big doctor's office variety and then some. Weigh-in scales are supposed to sit in the locker room, get certified once a year for accuracy, and never be moved even for cleaning because that might knock them off.

After Coach Fuzzball rolls his hairy round self out of the bus, a couple of his wrestlers unstrap the scale and start lugging it toward our gym. By now Coach Lindy has gotten the word. He saunters into the parking lot.

"Thought we'd help you out a little," Fuzzball tells him, "seeing as how the Maynard scale has been weighing heavy."

"Where'd you hear that?" This is no minor accusation. If a scale weighs heavy, guys who are right on weight look like they're over. Even if it's only a couple of ounces, they have to get rid of it before weigh-ins end or they can't wrestle. The skin above Coach Lindy's upper lip turns the chalky-white color it gets only when he's furious, but his expression stays neutral. He motions the Riverside wrestlers to put down the scale. He speaks in his most casual tone. "Who told you we were weighing heavy?" he asks Fuzzball again.

"Heard it around. Heard it from a couple of places."

Coach scratches the top of his bald head and pretends to be confused. "Now that puzzles me, Coach. It puzzles me because we just had our scale certified last month. Yes sir, the inspector said it was exactly right just a couple of weeks ago."

Fuzzball acts surprised. "Well, in that case." He signals his wrestlers to put the scale back in the bus.

"Looks like you'll have to have your own scale checked again after a trip like this," Coach Lindy says. "No telling what bumping over those roads could do to its balance."

His manner is still calm, but his face is a giveaway

red. He leans toward Fuzzball's furry head. "Why bother with weigh-ins at all if you're going to pull a stunt like this?" He waves toward the Riverside wrestlers standing by the bus. "What kind of lesson are you trying to teach them?"

At the weigh-ins, we see what this is all about. One of Riverside's best wrestlers doesn't make weight. He goes out and runs, but he's still a pound heavy. With so much of our team out, it's not going to make much difference in the final score, but Fuzzball didn't know we were short until just now. A slow smile creeps across his face as he registers our reduced numbers. "Looks like you're a little weak tonight," he tells Coach. "Even looks like Jake here hurt his shoulder."

Coach shrugs. "You think we look weak? I guess we'll see."

We have a couple of JV matches before the varsity meet. As a reward for hard work, and also to irritate Fuzzball, Coach Lindy lets Wanda Custer wrestle JV for the first time.

She snaps her headgear in place and warms up, running in place, jumping rope. Finally the ref signals her to approach. Fuzzball whispers a few words to his JV lightweight, a feisty kid everybody calls Tattoo. He's only fourteen and already has tattoos up and down both his arms. As he moves toward the mat, Fuzzball pats him on the butt.

When the whistle blows, Wanda starts to circle, but Tattoo doesn't budge, just smiles and waits. Wanda takes advantage and shoots. Tattoo doesn't resist. He lets her knock him off balance, drops, lets her push him to his back. Wanda might as well be wrestling a rag doll. The Riverside fans begin to laugh; some of our own fans join them. Two seconds later, Wanda has Tattoo pinned. The Maynard fans cheer, but the victory is a joke. When the ref raises Wanda's hand, Tattoo raises his own hand and shouts exuberantly to the crowd: "Rather lose by a pin than rassle some *girl*."

The other Riverside wrestlers hoot in support.

Wanda stomps away, pulls off her headgear, and slams it to the floor beside our bench. She grabs her gear bag and keeps walking. Coach starts after her, then stops and lets her go.

I figure it's up to me. I'm the one who created the monster. I take the ice pack off my shoulder and follow her to the corner of the gym, where she drops her bag, turns to face a set of folded-up bleachers, and starts pounding them with her fist.

"If this were the regular match instead of JV, slamming your headgear would cost us a point just like Marcus's crotch caper did last time," I tell her. "What's the matter with you?"

She stops pounding and turns to me, flushed and furious.

"At first I thought I could do it halfway, but no. You convince me it's got to be all or nothing. So I go all-out and the first time I get to wrestle, my opponent lays down. It's a joke. I'm a joke! What am I supposed to do, be ladylike and say, 'oh, sorry, I made a mistake?'"

"What did you expect, Wanda? Instant respect?"

"Well, I tried, didn't I? That's what you wanted me to do, wasn't it? *Wasn't it?*"

My shoulder cramps, sends out a twinge of pain. "You got it wrong, Wanda. I didn't want you to do anything. I didn't care what you did. I just told it like it was. Pole was working and you weren't. That simple."

"Well now I'm busting my butt. This isn't my fault. This isn't going to work."

"I could have told you that."

"Why didn't you?"

"I thought it was obvious."

"Biology is destiny, right?" she snarls.

I don't say anything.

"Oh, crap! I hated this from the beginning!"

"Then why didn't you quit?" I'm losing patience. My whole arm hurts, I'm worried about beating a Riverside guy I can usually pin without any trouble, and if anybody's biology is destiny, it's mine. If somebody's going to grouch, it should be me.

"I stayed with it because of *her*." She jerks her head in the direction of the upper bleachers.

"Who?"

"Ms. Macris."

"She's *here?*" The idea of The Mackerel at a wrestling match floors me. She hates "male-dominated" sports, hates jocks, hates anything that's not literary. I look up. Sure enough, there she is, sitting alone at the top of the bleachers, a grim expression on her face. What always stops me when I see her is that in my mind she's old and shriveled but in person she's young and not bad-looking – which is part of her power over people until they realize what she's like.

"The Mackerel told you to come out for wrestling?" I don't believe it.

"Yeah. She did. Okay? She *did*."

"Right. She's a real sports fan."

"She's a feminist. She thought it would be a good thing to write a paper on."

"You're doing this to write a paper?" I hear my voice rise with annoyance.

Wanda tugs at her singlet, looks uncomfortable. "She's big on essays. You know how she is."

"What a bunch of crap."

Wanda unzips her gear bag, pulls out a typed sheet of paper. "She even wrote an essay herself. On education. She's trying to get some teaching award. She's passing it out like candy." She thrusts the paper into my hand.

"What's that got to do with you?" I try to give the paper back, but Wanda won't take it. "You could have told her you hated wrestling and would write about something else."

Her face twists into a pout. "I couldn't quit. I couldn't. I didn't want to end up on her List."

"Her List!"

"*You* were on it. You didn't get into Honor Society." She takes a deep breath. "Listen, Jake, you got a scholarship anyway, you didn't need her. I do."

"You think Honor Society will get you a scholarship?"

"It won't hurt."

"Listen, if I got a scholarship without Honor Society, anyone can. Or you can go to school on loans and part-time work. It's not like you're going to have to give up your plans for college." All this is true. In recent days, these are issues I've been pondering deeply.

"You're a great one to talk." Wanda puts her hands on her hips, looks skeptical. "If it weren't for the ROTC scholarship, you'd probably get one for wrestling." She flares her nostrils, shoots me a sarcastic glance. "Not everyone has all your special talents."

The muscle in my shoulder goes into a spasm. I clench my teeth and wait for it to stop. I've had enough –and not just of the pain. "Listen, Wanda, wrestling is a minor sport. There aren't many scholarships. A lot of colleges are getting rid of wrestling altogether because it's an all-male sport and Gender Equity says you can't have more guys on scholarships than girls." I sound like I'm giving a lecture, but I don't care. "Wrestling gets dumped because it's not glamorous like football, and they add a woman's lacrosse team so they can give the money to girls. Don't tell me about wrestling scholarships! The only guys who still get them are the Lizard Smiths."

"Lizard Smith?"

"The guy who pinned his way to the state championship the last three years," I shout. "Who won the junior nationals two times in a row. The one everybody talks about at practice."

Wanda still looks baffled.

"The reason Marcus has no chance of winning the state," I tell her.

"Oh." She scratches her little bird-neck.

"If you were really so interested in wrestling, you'd know that."

Wanda pretends not to hear; she changes the subject. "I still can't believe Tattoo just laid over like that and made me a laughingstock."

"Stop whining, Wanda. Write your paper on the sexist wrestling behavior The Mackerel saw tonight and be done with it. Quit the team with dignity."

Wanda leans back against the wall, and when she speaks again, her voice is tinny. "She probably won't be happy with just a paper. She'll want me to lodge a protest or something."

"Well, that's up to you, isn't it? Ever hear of 'just say no'?"

Out on the mat, one of the JV's is getting pinned, and a roar goes up from the crowd. When it quiets down, Wanda says, "I don't want to be on her List."

Her lower lip juts out in a feeling-sorry-for-myself pose, and I'm so disgusted I don't remember why I ever came over here. "I don't believe what some people will do for their resumes," I say. The Mackerel's essay is still in my hand as I walk back to the bleachers. I crumple it up and dump it in my gear bag so Coach won't get on me about littering the floor.

• • •

Despite the fact that Riverside could crawl through this match and still beat us tonight, Fuzzball decides to make the evening as unpleasant as possible. He has his guys wrestle down-and-dirty even against our second stringers who've never wrestled varsity before. Riverside puts one of them into such a wicked banana split, with his legs pulled out so wide, that it looks like he's going to be torn in half. Riverside's fans stomp the bleachers as they watch our guy suffer. Riverside pulls out its nastiest moves, the ones that hurt most when you're on the receiving end. Before the night is over, the ref has called potentially dangerous or unnecessary roughness against Riverside half a dozen times. Despite my shoulder, I do all right against Evans. I don't pin him, but it wouldn't help if I had. Our team gets whomped.

I study the floor on the way to the locker room, hoping not to have to talk to anybody, when a figure bars my way. I look up into the round, fish-colored eyes of The Mackerel.

She doesn't smile or ask me how I am. She only shakes her head and says, with a slight, superior smile, "I'm glad I saw this with my own eyes. This is even more barbaric than I thought."

I consider telling her this isn't typical, but she wouldn't believe me so what's the point? She has no power over me now. I don't owe her anything. It takes all my willpower not to point out that barbaric things happen in her own classroom.

It crosses my mind that barbaric things have also happened to me personally since wrestling season began. More barbaric than tonight's wrestling match. Things she'd give her eye teeth to know but damn well never will. I shove past her and stomp my way into the locker room where she can't follow.

CHAPTER 20

The way Dad puts it later, I dream my way through the conference, dream my way through regionals. "You're just lucky it didn't turn out worse," he tells me.

When I think about it later, he's right. But at the time, I don't see it at all.

The end of the season rushes toward us – conference championships coming up the first week in February, regionals the following week. The guys on the team get over their stomach viruses. Workouts get tougher. Though it doesn't seem possible, Marcus comes back stronger than ever, and it's all I can do to beat him at practice. Afterwards I ice my shoulder just like the trainer tells me to. When Coach says, "Don't even think about lifting weights again until the season's over," I don't. But like Dad says, I'm dreaming.

Wanda Custer doesn't come to practice after the incident with Tattoo, and most of the wrestlers are relieved. To me it doesn't matter one way or the other. Mom doesn't reinstate my driving privileges even though the month's punishment is over. I don't care about that, either. Where would I drive, now that I've stopped lifting? My social life is nonexistent. The Great Liar is weary. He spends a lot of evenings in his room, listening to CDs, falling asleep early. It's easier not to slip up if you don't talk to anybody.

Chopper's the one with the social life these days.

He's made Margie a partner in his computer-research business, and although the two of them never touch unless their hands brush while they're trading printouts, at least he has someone to talk to. They even discuss The Mackerel's essay, which Chopper finds when I empty my gear bag. He uncrumples it and reads it all the way through. Then he reaches idly for his nonexistent glasses and says, "I've seen this before."

"Of course you've seen it," I tell him. "The Mackerel thinks it'll help her win some teaching award. She's proud of it. She's handed it out to half the school."

"Not to me," Chopper says. He gives it to Margie, who reads it and frowns.

"Yeah. Rings a bell," she says.

They shoot each other a meaningful look and then, without a word, walk over to the computer. Chopper types some words; Margie shakes her head. "Excellence in education?" she suggests. "Teaching methods?" Though I'm not quite following them, it's clear The Mackerel's essay has become their latest project. I doubt there's any real reason for this, doubt they've seen the essay before. It's just that they're always looking for something to do when they run out of paying clients. Something they can work on together.

They're a pair. It's weird, Chopper being part of a couple. Like Callie and I once were. But that seems long ago, part of another era. Life is simpler now. Workouts with the team. The long run home. Little pink pills three times a day. If there's a knot in my stomach, I don't notice it anymore. I might be watching myself on a video, for all I feel involved.

Except for the couple of days when I surface, look

around me, experience a little reality shock.

It begins when Marcus pulls his latest caper. He tells his English teacher he's going to the bathroom but instead heads for the gym and shoots baskets the rest of the period. To no one's surprise, this nets him in-school suspension the rest of the week. I ought to be relieved, not having to worry about him blabbing Jake's Big Secret. But more than I'm relieved, I miss him. His wrestling has improved a lot; practicing with him makes me better. Besides, it's been long time since I had my little "episode" in the motel room. I expected him to spread the word a long time ago, but so far he hasn't.

It occurs to me that maybe I could have trusted him.

And then I think: if I could have trusted Marcus, how about Callie? I picture her walking past me in the hallway, pretending not to notice me because she thought I broke up with her for no good reason. For the first time in days, I feel an honest, searing emotion: guilt. Even if there's going to be no happy ending for us, at least she deserves an explanation.

I head for her house right after practice, before I can lose my nerve. Wait on her porch nearly an hour before she gets home from chorus. She's so startled to see me, she almost drops her backpack. "I've got to talk to you," I blurt. She doesn't tell me to get lost, doesn't turn her back to me. "You must be freezing," she says.

Over calorie-free hot tea in her kitchen, I tell her everything. All the details, from day one, including turning down my scholarship before it gets taken away from me. Callie asks a couple of questions but doesn't gush. And doesn't seemed as horrified as I expected. "Did you really think it would make a difference?" she asks when I finish.

"Maybe not to you. But to me it does." I concentrate on the gray and brown stripes on my mug. I shred my tea bag, gather damp tea leaves into a little pile. "I couldn't have you staying because you feel sorry for me."

"Feel sorry for you! I was feeling sorry for myself because you dumped me!"

This is harder than I thought. "Don't you see? There's nothing I'd like better than for everything to be the same as it was before. But it's not. Not for me. Even if you didn't feel sorry for me, I'd worry that you did. It's not you I don't trust, it's myself. I can't help it."

Callie gathers our cups, takes them to the sink, stands there a long time. "I see," she whispers.

"What I mean is— " I clear my throat and start over. "What I mean is, the character flaw isn't yours, it's mine."

"I know." When she turns back to me, her green eyes are swimmy with tears. "I'm glad you told me. Knowing is better." She sniffs and wipes an eye. "It's not good, but it's better."

I have to get out of there. What I'm saying is true: I don't trust myself to trust her. I can't. If I stay longer, I might change my mind.

Instead of running home, I walk. It's freezing. All the better. I want to make sure I get cold enough to feel numb.

• • •

By the morning of conference championships, I'm back to feeling about as much emotion as a slab of concrete. Although the gym is crowded with nervous wrestlers, anxious parents, and a few girlfriends, it doesn't faze me a bit.

I chalk up an easy win early and prepare for a harder one later. My mouth isn't as dry as usual – always a good thing – but I have no feeling about that, either.

At the end of the day, it's even a struggle to psyche myself up for the championship round. This is the finals, I tell myself. The *finals*. I don't find my zone of concentration until the end of first period after my opponent reverses me and makes me mad. Then I wrestle well. Feel strong. Conference champ for the third time in a row! The crowd cheers; Chopper jumps up and down. Even Mom congratulates me with shining eyes. I note her expression, but everything's far away again – my own victory, Fuzzball's shenanigans with the refs, the way Marcus won his own championship with a tilt I didn't even think he knew. Afterwards, I realize that the only thing that captured my attention all day was what happened to Pole.

When you're a freshman, even one who's figured out a few things, you're not expected to do much at the conference level. But all day Pole keeps winning and advancing, which is a shock even though the number one lightweight is out with mono and the number two guy didn't make weight. In the semifinals, where we all expect Pole to lose, he squeaks by with one point for an escape in the last ten seconds. The whole Maynard team roars.

I figure what's got Pole keyed up is Coach's second-best speech, which he gives this time every year. "You can't let yourself settle for second best out there," he tells us. "And you know why? Because if you settle for second best now, you'll be doing it all your life. You'll settle for the second best job, the second best wife . . ." (If Wanda were still around we probably wouldn't hear the wife part) . . . "the second best life. Is that what you want?"

"No!" we yell back.

"I didn't catch that. Well? Is it?"

"No!"

I've heard this pep talk four times now and still can't figure out why Coach believes second best is not a factor "if you get beat honestly by a guy who's just plain better than you and you've done the best you can." But the younger guys always come away from this speech ready to grind the competition into the mat.

For the championship, Pole has to wrestle the same kid from Riverside he beat early in the season but didn't see again because he was out with the stomach virus. Riverside's lightweight is better than Pole. Worse, he's still angry at his defeat. Right off the whistle, he wrestles nasty. At the end of first period, he's up three to zip, and Pole looks like he won't last.

About ten seconds into second period, Riverside picks Pole up and starts carrying him around. Pole kicks and squirms but can't get free. Riverside's guy holds on. He moves to put Pole down. Instead of protecting Pole's back like he's supposed to, he slams him hard to the mat.

Coach Lindy leaps to his feet. "Blatantly illegal!" he yells as he rushes over. Pole lies dazed, in the exact position where he landed.

The ref calls injury time-out and waits to see if Pole will be able to continue. Pole shakes his head, tries to clear the fog, tries to get up.

"You have two minutes if you need it," Coach tells him. "Don't get up until you're ready. That's what injury time is for."

Fuzzball jumps up and storms at the ref. "He's telling his kid to lie down!" He points to Coach Lindy.

"He's telling him to lie down!"

What he means is, Coach is telling Pole to fake being more injured than he is, so they'll have to stop the match. If you're slammed illegally and can't go on, you're awarded the victory.

But it's clear Pole isn't faking. He's too groggy to go on even after two minutes. He staggers to his feet to let the ref raise his hand. He stumbles and then catches himself as he walks off the mat.

Fuzzball is furious, not with his wrestler like he ought to be, but with Coach. "You always do that?" he screams. "You always tell them to lie down?"

Coach's face flushes and the area above his lip turns chalky, but he doesn't respond. Times like these, his lectures about self-control come back and begin to sound not so cheesy.

He puts his arm around Pole and leads him towards us. Pole's still trying to clear his head. Coach beckons me to help Pole to the locker room.

Pole is so out of it he heads the wrong way. I steer him in the right direction.

"You won, buddy," I tell him. "You're conference champ. You're the man, buddy."

"Yeah?"

"Yeah, Pole."

"Well, you know, I figured I'd win," he says in a slurred, disjointed way. "I didn't want to be second best. I wanted to show 'em what the old Pole was made of."

"You did great, Pole." I point him towards his locker.

Just as Marcus' crotch caper hurt us early in the season, Pole's slam will help now. At the end of the night, for the first time in years, Maynard comes out conference champion, with Riverside in second place. The illegal move is what did it. If Riverside had wrestled fair, it probably would have gone the other way.

"We'll take it!" Marcus says as he flashes his own gold medal.

It isn't until the next day that the fun ends. We open our newspapers and see the interview with Fuzzball. He claims Maynard won only because Coach Lindy told his lightweight to lie down. That's when the victory begins to seem tainted.

• • •

By Monday, the accusations are all over radio and TV. Fuzzball tells all the reporters that Coach Lindy encouraged Pole to act injured so the match would be stopped. When asked, Fuzzball admits his own wrestler slammed Pole accidentally (accidentally!) – "But it's clear the boy could have gotten up if he wanted to. If his own Coach hadn't told him to lie there."

We're stunned. If anybody's cheating, it isn't us. Somebody gives a video of the championship matches to Channel 6, and we see Pole get slammed over and over again. There's no way he was faking. But the town is divided, and Fuzzball keeps doing every newspaper interview and talk show that will have him.

Coach Lindy tells the truth: all he did was advise Pole to take his full injury time if he needed it. Brian Fensel wants Coach to fight back, reveal Fuzzball's own stunts, like when he brought the scale to our gym. Coach refuses.

"If we leave it alone, it'll die," he says. "If I start making accusations, I lower myself to his level and end up in a pissing contest. Is that what you want?"

Maybe it is. For the first time, a whole week passes in February when wrestling gets more publicity than basketball. Our guys love it.

The only ones required to practice this week are those going on to regionals, but the rest of the team shows up, too. They offer to be workout partners for anyone who needs them. A bunch of prospects also show up, who say they'll be coming out next year. Even Wanda Custer wanders into the wrestling room one day. No one's glad to see her.

"I thought you quit," someone says.

"I just wanted to see how Pole was doing."

"He's fine."

In case she's planning to stay, I go up and explain, "The only people who have to practice now are the varsity guys who are going to regionals."

"I didn't come because I wanted to practice. After that fiasco with Tattoo, I knew Coach wouldn't let me wrestle again. Anyway it was almost the end of the season. Sometimes you have to know when to give it up."

"So did you write your paper for The Mackerel?"

She shakes her head. "She wanted me to do an article for the school newspaper, too. She wanted me to protest to some committee you can go to about discrimination. I told her it sounded like it was getting to be her cause, not mine."

"So much for Honor Society," I say.

"I might still make it."

"Don't count on it," I say. "Welcome to The List."

Wanda laughs. In her everyday clothes, jeans and a sweatshirt that comes to her knees, she looks smaller than in her workout clothes – like a miniature person, so small you wouldn't necessarily feel you had to take her seriously. I have an inkling this is why she wanted to make her mark as Maynard's first woman wrestler. It's almost sad. All the same, I'm glad when she leaves.

It's late, dark outside. Nobody's left in the wrestling room but those who have to be there. I focus on the smell of sweat, the grungy mats, the heat turned up to help us dehydrate a little weight. After a while I feel nothing except blood and muscles; I don't think about a thing. Like Dad says, I'm dreaming.

CHAPTER 21

Something I can't identify nags at the back of my mind all week. A hundred times I'm about to pinpoint it just as it slips away. By the time we're on the bus to regionals, it's driving me crazy. You'd think my main concern would be wrestling Colby Douglas in the finals (providing both of us get to the finals), or the fear I'll never be regional champ. But all I can think about is this elusive thing I can't get hold of.

Brian Fensel is in high form. He'll be happy if he makes it to states by getting one of the first four spots in his weight class, and he knows he has a good chance. He's full of jokes, though no more "Yo Momma" ones since the time Marcus almost strangled him.

"See, this lady comes home from work and finds her dog lying in the driveway, not breathing," he tells us, "so she rushes him to the vet. And the vet tells her he's dead. But she says, 'Doctor, are you really sure? How can you be certain?'

"The vet says wait a minute, we'll do one more thing. So he brings in this cat. The cat walks all around the dog sniffing at every part of him – paws, ears, belly, everything." Brian makes a few sniffing noises. "Then they take the cat away and the vet says, 'Lady, the dog's really dead. There's nothing we can do.'

"So the lady goes home and when the bill comes, it's

for two hundred dollars. She's shocked. She calls the office and says it's too much, it must be a mistake. The vet says, 'It's no mistake, lady. It was fifty dollars for my examination and the other hundred and fifty for the cat scan.'"

Everybody laughs, even Marcus – everybody but me. I never had a CAT scan, but I had an MRI, and right now it doesn't seem like something to joke about.

What's wrong with me?

Wrestling starts that afternoon and continues through the next day. Most of the younger guys don't make it past the first round. Before long all that's left is me, Marcus, Brian Fensel, and Brunson. All the seniors.

Once guys who've been eliminated get over being disappointed, usually they have a good time. Their season's over; they can eat and fool around. The only one who doesn't join in the fun is Pole. He didn't make it very far, and he's still upset even after Coach tells him it doesn't matter. "Just experiencing this level of wrestling is going to help you," Coach says.

"Right," Pole sulks when I try to console him. "Remember at the beginning of the season when Coach said the best I could do was go from super-sorry to sorry? I guess he wasn't kidding."

"If you were sorry you wouldn't be at regionals at all."

"I wouldn't be here if I hadn't gotten slammed."

"Listen, Pole, next year you'll be better. It's like crawling through a cave. It's a squirmy sort of thing. You're always feeling your way. You wiggle through and feel for them to get a little off balance, and then you squirm through the little hole they make. You'll learn more. You've learned a lot already."

He stops glowering and nods as if this makes sense. To me it sounds like babble. The nagging feeling – more like dread by now – gnaws at my gut. I find a place under the bleachers and nurse it until Dad finds me and asks me if I want to go out to eat.

"No, I wrestle again in a couple of hours."

"Let's go for a walk. It'd be good for you to get out of here for a while."

"I'm okay," I tell him. Mom and Chopper couldn't get away, so Dad drove up and stayed in a motel by himself last night. He probably wants company. But I don't want to go anywhere or talk to anyone. I want stay under the bleachers and take a nap.

Marcus and I are the only two who make it to the finals. Marcus hasn't been regional champion before, either. Last year, when I came in second, he got fourth – just good enough to make it to states. This year, as soon as he knows he's in the finals, he's more antsy than I've ever seen him. The man-of-no-nerves paces the floor, can't sit still, keeps pinching and rubbing the ear with his lucky earring. "Gold stud," he tells me three different times as he caresses it. He says it the way you'd say *abracadabra* or *ohm*, a chant to charm him into winning.

When he says *gold stud*, Marcus doesn't mean just the earring, which actually is a gold stud but nothing remarkable. He means the victorious gold stud he believes he himself can be as long as the earring is his touchstone. Strange reasoning, but I don't argue since I still carry my lucky T-shirts in my gear bag even though I don't wear the Marine Corps Bad to the Bone anymore and can hardly look at the stupid pink tie-dye shirt Callie gave me.

By the time Marcus goes out for his championship

round that evening, I've been trying to warm up for half an hour. I wrestle right after he does, but I still feel like a robot. My body's stiff, my hands are cold, and it doesn't help that Colby Douglas looks like he's grown a foot since the last time I saw him. Worse still is the nagging unease that's hung over me all day. I start doing jumping jacks; I jog in place and raise my knees high to get my heart pumping. All at once, like someone's turned on the light, my body heats up and my mind shifts gears. And finally I know what's bothering me.

It's Coach's second-best speech.

It's the way I suddenly realize what that speech is describing.

Me.

Second best, second string, second rate, second class.

Jake Chapman, always such a winner. But not really. Not anymore.

I stop jogging, stand in place like I'm glued there. What's the point of all this if it doesn't make any difference whether I win? I'll still be unfit for the military. Unfit to drive. Not good enough for a ROTC scholarship. Epileptics are second best. Unfit to live the first-class life of people who are normal.

And there's nothing I can do about it.

Nada.

This is the fact I've been trying to avoid.

No wonder.

This is why I've been dreaming.

A roar goes up. Marcus wins! He comes off the mat glistening with sweat and joy. I'm still too locked inside myself to move. Great timing, Jake. The exact wrong second to come to terms with reality. But there I am. It doesn't matter that I'm about to go after the regional championship. Not anymore. Not now. All that matters is my feeling that I've already lost.

No wonder I get out there and wrestle like a clumsy freshman. No wonder I forget Coach's advice to stay on my feet. The only wonder is that I lose by three points instead of five or six.

Coach's expression is stony when I come off the mat. "Your body was there, but the rest of you didn't show up."

I start to say something but he raises a hand. "We'll talk about it Monday."

Brian Fensel says what the hell, you made it to states, you get another chance next week. Brian made it himself: fourth. And Brunson, who got third, tells me I'll do it next time.

Marcus says, "Sorry, man," and cuffs me on the shoulder. But he's a champion, he's happy; why should he care?

Dad comes up last. He's not smiling. "Don't go back on the bus," he says. "I want you to ride with me."

Which is worse? Having to rehash the match on the bus with guys who'll tell me it was bad luck but who all know I wrestled like crap? Or having to rehash it with Dad, who'll analyze it move by move all the way home?

Dad at least keeps his mouth shut until the next town where we stop for dinner. It's a buffet. We load up our plates and pretend we're too busy eating to talk. I wish Chopper were there to lighten the mood. Finally Dad clears his throat a couple of times. "You could have won tonight, Jake," he says. "I think you know that."

"Once somebody sticks legs, you don't just wiggle out real easy," I mumble. This is something I never do – make excuses.

"You didn't fight him off. You know that."

"Yeah. All right. I didn't." I drain a glass of water so I won't have to look at him.

"You know what your problem is? You're cocooning. You've been doing it for weeks. It's destructive. It's taking its toll." He lifts his root beer, then sets it down.

"You want to define cocooning?" I ask.

"It's what people do when they're cold – huddle into themselves, go off alone and hug themselves to get warm. But it can also mean spending half your day hiding under the bleachers, turned in on yourself. Or spending all your time lifting weights and running so you won't have to face anybody." He meets my eyes for just a second, then runs his finger across his frosted mug, draws a squiggly line.

"See, when you're cold you want to get off alone to make yourself feel better, but what actually happens is, you sit there and think how miserable you are. You're not warm. If it's cold enough, you're not going to get warm. You'd do better to stop thinking about it and go talk to people instead. It's a term I learned when we were out in the field in the Marines. Some Major came over and told me to stop cocooning. Made me stop feeling sorry for myself."

"The all-wise Marines," I say.

"I always thought they were wise." He shrugs. "You never cared much about them."

"Right, Dad." I make my tone arch and skeptical.

Dad ignores it. "You wouldn't even have applied for that scholarship if I hadn't suggested it," he says. "Think about it. It was never really your dream, it was Chopper's."

"Chopper's!"

The door to the restaurant opens and two kids rush in and scramble toward a booth in the corner, followed by their parents. When the commotion dies down, I say, "Chopper's dream isn't to be a Marine, it's to take over Microsoft by the time he's twenty."

"Maybe now it is. But remember when he used to go around making those helicopter noises?"

"He was just a little kid."

Dad doodles some more on the side of his mug and says slowly, "He was helicopter-crazy until fifth grade."

"Yeah. Then he decided he hated his teacher and stopped doing schoolwork until you got him that computer. It had nothing to do with helicopters."

"Fifth grade was when he got his glasses. When he knew his eyes were going to be bad."

"So?"

"He stopped doing school work because he knew he was never going to be a helicopter pilot."

"Far-fetched, Dad. He just hated his teacher."

"I don't think so. He was young, but he wasn't stupid. He knew you needed perfect vision to fly. He came up to me and said, 'I can't be a pilot anymore, can I?' And when I told him no, but there were other things he could be, he just walked off. Gave up on school and everything else." Dad taps his chest in the neighborhood of this heart. "It hurt."

The waitress comes over with the check. I wait for her to leave before I whisper, "If flying was his big dream and he gave it up, why did you keep buying those Marine Corps shirts for him? Why did he keep wearing them?"

"I didn't buy those shirts for a long time. Not until

he got his computer and flying didn't matter to him anymore," Dad whispers back. "Once he got the computer, his life had a different direction."

"Yeah, and now he's Arnold Schwarzenegger with a computer-nerd girlfriend."

Why are we whispering? Self-consciously, Dad clears his throat again. "The point is, Chopper was the one who saw himself in the uniform, not you."

I shake my head to show how unlikely this sounds. But there's a grain of truth in it. I never pictured myself leading a bunch of men up a mountain or through the jungle the way Chopper pictured himself flying that helicopter. When I pictured anything, it was me at the wrestling finals, me with my hand raised high in victory.

Is Dad trying to tell me that's still an option? The state championships are next week. But since the season started the main thing I've done is lose: scholarship, driving privileges, girlfriend. Maybe The Mackerel knew something I didn't when she kept me out of Honor Society. I'm second rate. I can't change it any more than I can stop the weird firing of neurons inside my brain.

Maybe I am cocooning. And maybe I don't care.

"Listen, Jake," Dad says as if he's following my thoughts. "You could have played tennis or baseball and I would have been just as happy for you. But you took to wrestling. It was all you wanted to do." He picks up the check, fishes his wallet from his pocket. "You can write off the Marines and a lot of other things because you don't care about them. But don't write *this* off."

Despite the muted amber light of the restaurant, everything looks especially clear: the features of the other customers, the scraps of food on the plates that haven't been cleared, the zig-zag pattern of tiles on the floor. So clear it's painful. Like a scab being torn off from in front of my eyes.

Who am I kidding?

I do care.

I'm not dreaming.

No longer numb.

This is worse.

This is a slow burn, fire under every inch of my skin. A hot blue flame of rage.

CHAPTER 22

Sunday night Chopper beckons me into his room to show me something on the computer.

"What?" I don't care what he's researching. I'm still burning. Wishing I could crawl back into my cocoon. Filled with blue fury.

"Read this," Chopper orders. He points to a paragraph about the value of individual attention for students in a class. Hardly a riveting topic.

"So?"

Chopper picks up a wrinkled paper from his desk, which I recognize as The Mackerel's essay. There's a paragraph in it exactly like the one on the screen.

"Plagiarism," he says.

"What?"

He types a few strokes and brings up another paragraph, also identical to one of The Mackerel's. This one's about making your students set high goals. "She's not stupid," he says. "She didn't take it all from one place."

"What do you mean?"

"She lifted the essay she's so proud of from three different articles by three different education hot-dogs. Not recent ones, either. These essays were published fifteen years ago."

I'm speechless – not because The Mackerel might do a crummy thing like plagiarize, but because Chopper's smart enough to catch her.

"Jesus," I say. "Who would have thought."

"Yeah, this stuff is pretty obscure. Only reason I found it is because Margie and I researched a paper for a kid writing about school systems."

"Cyber-detective," I say. "Cyber-stud."

He nods, satisfied. "So, what are you going to do?"

"What do you mean?"

"I mean, to nail her."

My slow burn intensifies. "Nail her? What's the point? A year ago, yes— but now?"

"What's the point!"

"This spring I graduate. I'm out of here. She never happened." I turn on him as if he's personally responsible for all my pain. "You want to nail her, do it yourself."

Chopper shakes his head. "What a wuss," he says.

• • •

The next day Mom tells me to take the car to school. She's humoring me by letting me drive, but I don't care. It's been months since my last seizure.

"I'm doing this so you can take Chopper to the Y after practice," she says. "I'm not sure I'll be home from work in time to do it."

Right. Give the spazz-boy a crumb. But when she holds out the keys, it's all I can do not to snatch them from her hand.

Coach has rounded up a couple of guys from the other high school in town – not Riverside – to work out with the four of us who are going on to states. But first he draws me aside and gives me the lecture I've been bracing for all day: if you don't want it, you're not going to get it; whatever happened to focusing? whatever happened to doing your best? I thought I was prepared to hear this, but still it stings.

Half an hour into the workout a couple of older guys come into the wrestling room to watch, but I'm too busy drilling to pay much attention. Then we stop and see who it is: somebody I know only as The Blind Guy, and his friend. Until he graduated last year, The Blind Guy wrestled for a school about an hour away. He was good, made it to states twice. Coach stops the drill and brings him over. "Guys, you remember this little fella, don't you?"

"Yeah, sure," we all say. The Blind Guy isn't little.

Coach turns in my direction. "Jake," he says, "Between now and the state tournament, this is your workout partner."

The Blind Guy's specialty, everyone knows, is riding legs.

The angry flame that's been with me since Saturday rises a notch. Though he was never in my weight class, I remember the special rule they had for wrestling The Blind Guy. It was that you had to stay in physical contact with him the whole time. Otherwise he had no way of knowing where you were. But this meant there was almost no way to shoot on him. My low single is going to be worthless.

Which I soon realize is exactly the point.

We drill for what seems like forever. The Blind Guy twists me into braids I haven't had to endure since I was a freshman. The fact that he outweighs me doesn't help. It's humiliating. Coach keeps stopping it, then explaining what I should do like I'm a beginner.

"As long as his hips are higher than yours, he's in control. You've got to find some way to sit. Then get his butt on the mat. Then attack his leg. Think about the snake that's slithering toward you. Man-eating. Inches away."

Right. Every time we start again, I know just how Pole felt when he said the most the snake could do for him was make him wiggle his toe. Coach is making a laughing-stock out of me not only in front of Marcus and Brian and Brunson, but in front of a bunch of guys from another school. By the time we leave practice I'm out for blood.

The only blood being shed these days is my own.

Chopper's waiting at home to go lift weights. I fling the door open and motion him into the car.

"Rough day?"

"If you want a ride, get in. *Now*."

"If it was such a hardship, you should have said so."

I send him a withering glance. Two months ago, he would have flinched. Now he only says, "Scary, Jake. You're very scary."

My own brother thinks I'm a wuss.

Talk about adding insult to injury, when I drop Chopper at the Y, who's standing right outside the door but my old buddy, Wanda Custer. I want to pretend I don't see her, but she waves and asks how I'm doing.

"Fine, Wanda. You need a ride?" I figure she's already waiting for someone; I expect her to say no.

"Sure," she says. "Great."

Great. She tells me where she lives. It's out of the way. "What brings you to the Y?" I ask.

She does a double-take, as if to suggest my mental capacities have diminished since the last time we met. "Lifting weights. Like always."

"Oh."

"You thought I quit, didn't you?"

"No, I—" But she's right. I thought she gave it up

when she gave up wrestling.

"I never liked wrestling, but I kind of like lifting. I'm getting a lot stronger. I still run, too."

"Yeah? Well, good."

"I'll probably go out for track this spring. I know I'm late getting started, but I might try anyway." She has this annoying hopeful lilt to her voice.

Dilettante, I think – Coach's unflattering term for people who go from one sport to another without getting serious about any of them. Wanda annoys me as much as ever.

We sit through two lights in rush hour traffic before we can turn into her subdivision. I can't wait to drop her off. It's all I can do to be polite. Struggling to make conversation, I ask her how she's doing with The Mackerel.

"Oh, great. Just dandy. She even gave me the pig-face treatment." She laughs.

"You think it's funny?" I remember walking into The Mackerel's room last year and finding the dreaded paper pig-face on my desk. I remember everyone's snickers, remember convincing myself it was one of Life's Little Lessons. "It isn't funny. You ought to complain."

"Right. Like Karen Russell complained." Touché. When Karen told Mr. Bodie about the pig-face, he didn't believe her. Mr. Bodie is The Mackerel's greatest supporter. Wanda shrugs. "Maybe I'm resigned."

"Like you're going to be resigned when you don't get into Honor Society?"

"What do you expect me to do about it?" Her voice rises; I've touched a nerve. "What did you ever do when it happened to you? You made it into a big joke!"

"Relax, Wanda."

Before this can go further, she points to a low-slung brick house at the end of the street. "Right there." I hit the brakes and barely stop before she bolts out and disappears.

Great, Jake, now she hates you.

Why should I care?

But I think about Chopper's discovery on the Internet all the way to pick him up at the Y.

And I think how he called me a wuss.

• • •

One thing I discover is, you work more efficiently at a slow burn. I don't even form a plan; the plan seems to have been there all the time, waiting for me to pluck it out of the air.

Even so, if it weren't for the fire in my gut, I'm not sure I could do it. That night I call a select group from last year's List and ask them to help me. Not one of them says no. I'm set.

What I don't expect is for Callie to corner me on my way to lunch the next day and steer me into the library. "I heard about the calls you made," she says in an accusatory voice. "Why wasn't I included?"

"You got into Honor Society. You don't have a beef."

"You can't believe that." She points us toward a table back by the stacks. "Remember when we sat in the auditorium decided not caring would be the best revenge? Of course we cared. It was one of the worst days of my life. When I think about it, it still hurts. Even now." She takes a deep breath. "The Mackerel's doing it again, isn't she?"

I nod. "She's got her List, she's got her pig-face out . . . she's treating people like they were slugs in her garden."

"Are we talking about somebody specific?"

"Wanda Custer. That girl who came out for the wrestling team."

Callie jerks her head back and shoots me a startled look. "*She's* your new love interest?"

"Jesus, Callie!" I'm honestly shocked. "You don't really think that!"

Callie shrugs.

The librarian cranes her head around the corner and shushes us. I drop my voice to a whisper. "What happened between you and me had nothing to do with Wanda or any other girl. You know that."

After what seems like an hour, Callie nods. "I guess I do." She leans forward to hear me better. "What are you going to do?"

I reach into my backpack and pull out the essay and the printouts from Chopper's computer. I explain everything. Callie reads all the papers, gives them weighty consideration.

"I'm taking these to Mr. Bodie," I tell her.

Callie frowns. "Even when he sees it, he'll defend her some way. He'll make it . . . not a big deal."

"That's why I'm sending it to the newspaper, too. And the radio and TV stations. One thing I learned from Fuzzball, it's the power of the press."

"TV and radio are—" she begins.

"I mean, not just me. Meg O'Malley and Jason Wilson and Terry Parkhurst—"

"And me," she says decisively. "If everyone who complains is someone who didn't get into Honor Society, it'll sound like sour grapes. But if I go with you— If I—"

"Do some of the talking?"

Callie's green eyes open about a mile wide.

"I mean, you've been in chorus so long. You don't get nervous." Why am I babbling?

Callie takes a long breath, then goes dead calm the way Mom always does in a crisis. "Sure. If I'm going to get into this, why not get in all the way?"

I open my mouth to thank her, but she raises her hand.

"I'm not doing this for you, Jake. I've thought about this a lot. I'm not doing it for revenge, either. I'm doing it because I remember how The Mackerel made me feel and I want her to stop. I'm doing it because I want justice."

"Yeah, me, too." Then I remember something else. I pull it from my backpack, slide it toward Callie across the table. "If plagiarism doesn't nail her, you can always use this."

Callie actually smiles.

• • •

The Blind Guy has a name: Gary Hanson. He's in his second year at the community college, and next year he'll probably transfer to State.

"I help coach a wrestling club to keep in shape," he tells me. "I try to work out every day."

"I can tell," I say.

"You're better than you think you are," he replies.

Maybe it's because he's blind that Gary never loses his concentration. Maybe because he's older. Or because he's just good.

We touch hands, we circle. I can't shoot because I'd have to stop touching him to do it. He stalks me; he pounces, gets me down, rides my legs like a cowboy.

"Hips," Coach keeps repeating. "You can reach back and grab his hip and sit. Or you can back into him. You might even be able to roll into it. But you've got to sit."

We do it a thousand times.

He's like a cat. But a blind one. How can this keep happening?

After the second thousand times, I get so I can sit.

"Now attack his leg! Get your arm underneath his knee!"

Which is just fine, except while I'm attacking his leg, he's trying to take my head off. Which hurts.

"Turtle your neck up as hard as you can! Suck it up, keep working! If you're not tough, he'll pull you right back and pin you."

So I've noticed.

I tuck my neck; I let Gary smash my nose; we're having a grand old massacre. Finally I get a hand under his knee, and it holds me.

Coach blows the whistle. "See?" He's elated. "If you're tough enough, all he should be able to do is put the hurts on you. He shouldn't be able to pull you back."

"Only the hurts, how comforting," a voice says. We turn around. The Mackerel stands in the doorway, arms crossed like she's trying to hold in an explosion.

"I think somebody wants to talk to you, Jake," Coach says.

I pick up a dry T-shirt and put it on as slowly as I can before I walk over to her. She holds the papers I took to the principal's office at lunch time. Her round fish-eyes blaze. "I understand you're behind this."

I shrug, hold her gaze.

"If you thought I was doing something dishonest,

Jake, don't you think you should have come to me personally before going over my head?"

"Don't you think you should have come to me personally about my unworthiness before you blackballed me from Honor Society?"

"That's ridiculous. One teacher can't—"

"Are you saying you didn't plagiarize?" I try to make my words come out in a lazy drawl like Coach does when he's playing mind-games with Fuzzball.

"If I did, it was unintentional," she says. "Sometimes you read something that impresses you so much that years later, without knowing it, you use exactly those words, those phrases—"

"Bullshit, Ms. Macris," I say.

Her face is a mask, no emotion at all. "All the same, that's exactly what happened."

"You think Mr. Bodie's going to buy that?"

She stands up straighter. "You know what I think, Jake? I think you're trying to take revenge for— For all these things you imagine I've done to you— For—"

"Not an issue," I say.

Seconds pass. We have a staring contest. She looks away first. "I see," she says. "Then I guess I'll see you tomorrow." Which is when Mr. Bodie has instructed us to meet with him in the principal's office.

What The Mackerel doesn't know is, the show is going to begin just a little bit sooner.

• • •

The next morning, the story is on "Sunrise" on Channel 6 TV. The anchor reads part of The Mackerel's essay and parts of Chopper's printouts. She says the similarities were discovered by an unnamed computer student. She says Ms. Macris could not be reached for comment.

"As to reaction from Ms. Macris's former students, we go to reporter Andrea Gale, live at Maynard High School." In front of the school in the early-morning cold, the reporter is surrounded by Jason, Meg, Terry, and Callie.

"What was your reaction to the possibility of plagiarism?" Andrea asks. "Shock?"

"Not really," Jason Wilson tells her.

"She was very hard on some of her students," Meg says. "Not everybody, but a certain few. She isn't what you'd call a fair person."

The reporter lifts a mock-up of the pig-face into the camera's view – the one Chopper created on his computer that looks exactly like The Mackerel's original. The one I gave Callie in the library.

"Kind of funny-looking," the anchor says.

"Not when you walk into class and find it on your desk," Callie says. She explains that Ms. Macris has certain ways to humiliate students she doesn't like – the same students who never get into Honor Society, even if they're in the top ten in the graduating class. "I was one of them myself," she says. "I didn't get in until I was out of her class."

The anchor grows serious. "You're putting a lot on the line here."

"It's a relief to have it in the open." The camera moves in on Callie's face, which is perfectly serene. "It's not hard to believe she was dishonest," she says.

I get to school early for my meeting with Mr. Bodie, but The Mackerel's already there. If she's upset about the publicity, she hides it well. She's sweetness itself. If she's done something that looks like cheating, she hopes we'll understand it was purely unintentional. She didn't copy from those articles; she must have unconsciously memorized things that affected her deeply. She turns to me and makes her voice gentler yet. "I know some of you don't believe this, Jake," she says. "But I never blackballed anyone from Honor Society. All I ever did – all I had the *authority* to do – was speak my mind." She lowers her gaze, the picture of modesty. I sense she's rehearsing her performance.

Outside the office, Jason, Meg, and Callie are waiting to hear what happened.

"She's going to be pretty effective," Callie says when I tell them. "Mr. Bodie probably won't do anything. She'll defend herself and lot of people will believe her."

"Maybe, but I don't think it'll do her any good." I lift my hands as if to frame a headline. *'Students Accuse Teacher of Plagiarism, Favoritism.'* What's she going to say?"

"Not much," Jason says. "She can't discredit all of us."

Everyone nods. At the very least, The Mackerel's going to be running scared from now on. Too scared to make a List.

Meg and Jason move off, but Callie lingers.

"I think we did it," she says wistfully.

"I think we did." I touch her hand for what we both know might be the last time, and she holds it for a while before letting go. "Thanks, Callie," I say.

• • •

At wrestling, Gary and I practice riding legs another thousand times. "The best thing is to stay on your feet," Coach keeps saying. "But a good guy always seems to find some way in."

Which Gary does. Every time. I hold on; I sit back into him, get my hand under his knee, rip on his ankle with my other hand, try to forget he's trying to remove my face feature by feature.

"Okay, now begin to walk on your butt away from him," Coach yells. "Scooch away! Get away from his hips!"

Another thousand times. I scooch away.

I've practiced this before. My whole four years here. But never this often. Not in slow motion. Not against a guy who's blind but ten times better than me, when I'm not even handicapped! *Not even handicapped!* I keep the leg, put space between us. I hold on.

"Okay, now rotate," Coach says. "If you keep hold of his leg, he has to come with you. Move, Jake! *Work.*"

As I start to rotate, an amazing thing happens: I feel myself going from defense to offense. I flip to my belly. If Gary holds on, he's pinned.

He lets me go.

CHAPTER 23

The first time you go to the state tournament, it's not just awesome, it's terrifying. Nine mats, a zillion wrestlers from all three divisions. And every one of them good enough to crush your average wrestler like a roasted peanut. Even though it's double elimination – you have to lose twice – it's easy to get so intimidated that you go two and out the first day. That's what I did as a sophomore, and what Marcus has done twice. Brunson squeaked through to the second day last year but then lost early that morning. Brian Fensel has never been here before. First thing he does when we get to the coliseum Thursday night to check our weight, he takes off his shirt so everyone can see the tattoo of a bloody knife he had put on his left bicep over the holidays. Mr. Macho.

Our motel is the usual rundown fleatrap with paper-thin walls and stains on the rug, but at least Marcus is my only roommate. We're both hyper, though Marcus pretends not to be. He throws his bag on his bed like he's annoyed at something else entirely and says, "All I hope is, you brought your pills this time. I got too much on my mind to share my room with the Fits Man."

The Fits Man? A shiver of anger runs through me, but I blow it off. I remove a plastic baggie from my pocket and hold it up to show the supply of little pink tablets. "You're safe, Marcus." I unzip my gear bag and pull out a bottle of the same pink pills. I open my shaving kit and unwrap a folded-up square of tin foil with more of the pills tucked inside.

Marcus laughs.

"Boy Scout training. Be prepared."

"I don't see you as a Boy Scout, man." He hoots but doesn't relax. For once he's as antsy as I am. Which is plenty.

We're not the only ones. Next morning before the wrestling starts, the whole coliseum smells like nervous sweat. I warm up forever to make sure I don't stiffen up, and so does Marcus. Both of us win. That means we don't have to wrestle again until the quarterfinals that evening. But neither of us calms down. I watch Colby Douglas tear up his own opponent, and after that I'm aware of him all day like something crawling under my skin. Marcus paces the floor like a caged panther.

By the middle of the afternoon, Brian is out and Brunson has lost once. The rounds follow each other in rapid succession. No breaks, no easy matches to loosen you up and make you feel good. When Brunson finally loses the second time, he actually looks relieved. Soon as he cools down, he opens his bag, takes out a package of cheese crackers, starts munching down.

It seems like forever before we get to the quarterfinals. Marcus and I both win. Not with the greatest wrestling of our careers, and not by much. But it doesn't matter. We've made it to the semifinals the next morning.

I hold my breath as I check the pairings. Colby also won in the quarterfinals. I'm relieved to see we're not matched up in the semis. I'm up against a guy named Kevin West from the other part of the state. He's good, but he's not

Colby.

Marcus isn't so lucky. In the semifinals, he'll be facing Lizard Smith, who hasn't lost once his whole high school career.

• • •

Back at the motel, Marcus and I both call home. Dad's plan was to come up for tomorrow's matches as long as I'm still in the running. It's a four-hour drive, a long way. Marcus' mother says she'll come if she can.

"If she can," Marcus says bitterly. "You know what that means."

"Wait and see. She might show."

"Yeah, give her the benefit of the doubt." He fingers his ear, gets a dark expression on his face.

"What's wrong?"

He pulls on his earlobe like he's about to detach it. "Jesus Christ!" he says.

"Marcus, what?"

Then I see. The earlobe is bare. No lucky earring.

He unhands his ear and grabs his gear bag, dumps it on the floor. He rips through it so fast he wouldn't find the earring if it was right in front of him.

"Relax, Marcus. Think. Who'd you give it to before you wrestled?"

He empties the bag in a panic – jock strap, T-shirt, disposable razor. "I didn't give it to anybody. I put it on the bleachers."

"Then it's probably still there."

"Get real, Fits Man."

I'd say something about the nickname if there were any chance Marcus would listen. But he's spazzing out, and he's got a genuine problem. His earring is small, the coliseum is large; the earring is valuable (sort of), and items of value disappear if you don't keep your eye on them. Marcus lifts his singlet from the bag, searches the bottom with his fingers, throws everything back inside.

"Don't you have two earrings?" I ask. "Where's the other one?"

"At home."

"Call your mother back. Let her bring it up."

He flings his gear bag toward the wall. "She's not gonna bring it. She's not coming!"

"Yeah, well my mother's not coming either. So what? We're not three years old."

"Your father's coming. Your brother'll probably come. Shit, even The Blind Guy said he'd come."

"He's not The Blind Guy. His name is Gary. You gonna start calling me The Fits Man now? Is that it? I'm the Fits Man and he's the Blind Guy? And what are you? The Spazzmeister?"

He's too far gone to be insulted. "Last time I didn't have the earring that guy from Westover put me in a grapevine and nearly broke my leg!" he yells.

"The grapevine was two years ago! You think it was because of the earring?"

"You think it wasn't?" He comes close, gets right in my face. "Now I get Lizard Smith in the semis. How do you know it wasn't the earring?"

He shoves me in the chest, not hard. He's so spastic, I let it go.

"What do *you* know?" he says. "For me, this is it, man. For you, this is just one little blip on your radar. You got college, you got your scholarship, you got your life, man. When I graduate, I got the streets. I got nothing."

He shoves me again, and this time I shove back. "Yeah, I got my life, but I sure as hell don't have my scholarship. You get to be the Fits Man and it's over." I shove him again, harder.

He reels back, hits his shoulder against the wall. "What do you mean . . . over?" he shouts. "Don't give me no shit, man. Don't humor me. Don't give me no—" He lunges for my chest; I push him away. This time he hits the wall with a mighty clunk.

"I mean no scholarship, no Marines, no way," I shout as he launches himself in my direction. "The deal is off, close the door, zip up your pants, good night, the fat lady sings."

With that, he lands on me. Next thing I know we're in a regular shoving contest. The wall's our backboard, we're the ball. It takes a while before the pounding on the door catches our attention.

We stop. Gasp for breath, straighten our shirts. Marcus opens the door. Coach stands outside, hands on his hips. His face is crimson.

"What going on here?"

"Nothing," we say in unison.

"Nothing?" Coach saunters over to the wall, runs his fingers across it to check for dents and scuffs. "A little disagreement?"

"It was nothing, Coach," I say.

"Nothing important," Marcus adds

"Good." Coach retreats to the doorway, glances from one of us to the other. "Save your hostility for the semis," he drawls. "You're gonna need it." He closes the door behind him.

Marcus and I stand in the middle of the room, catching our breath. "You really lost the scholarship?" he asks finally.

I nod.

"Why didn't you tell me?"

"All I'm saying is, living in the projects isn't the friggin end of the world, Marcus."

"And being the Fits Man is?"

"Yeah, it is." I drop onto my bed. "No, it isn't. But it's close."

Marcus remembers his earring, puts his finger to his earlobe, massages it the way Aladdin must have rubbed his lamp to make the genie appear. "You don't know, man." He doesn't sound angry anymore, only sad. I figure no way his mother's going to show up. I figure no way will he graduate this spring without another couple of trips to the Alternative School. I figure no way can he beat Lizard Smith, even if they wrestle a hundred times.

"I don't think it's the earring that gives you luck, Marcus," I tell him. "I don't think it depends on that earring."

"Yeah, don't I wish."

I get up, find my gear bag, and pull out my Bad to the Bone shirt which I haven't worn for months but didn't have the heart to leave at home. "What it depends on, man," I say as I hand it to Marcus, "is this."

• • •

Coach always says the semifinals are the most interesting round of the state tournament because guys are willing to take chances to get to the finals. "If you lose the championship, you're still number two in the state," he says.

"But if you lose in the semis, you never get the shot at the title."

Although we've heard this many times, Coach refrains today out of respect to Marcus. What he does say he directs to me and Marcus both: "Your objective is to wrestle the best you can – same objective as always. Focus on that and forget everything else. You only see the obstacles when you take your eye off the goal."

It just so happens that Coach says this while I'm watching Colby Douglas warm up about two feet away from me. I make myself stop. Next to me, Marcus keeps fingering thc skull on the Bad to the Bone T-shirt the way he used to finger his earring. So much for his calm African-American blood.

Brunson tries to calm him down. "Not many guys get this far, Marcus. I didn't. Doesn't matter what happens. Enjoy it." Inasmuch as Brunson is a football player and something of Marcus's hero, this should help, but it doesn't.

Fensel takes a different approach. "This is a *Rocky* situation, man," he says as he flexes his bicep to make his bloody-knife tattoo look larger. "Remember the first *Rocky* movie? Same deal here. Go the distance and don't get pinned."

Marcus stops fidgeting. None of us would have predicted Fensel, who's better at jokes than deep thoughts, would save the day, but Marcus brightens. Suddenly he's a man with a plan. When his match comes up, he goes the distance and only loses by one. We're all amazed, Marcus most of all.

Compared to that, my own match is anticlimactic. I win six to three. Colby wins his own semifinal match by exactly the same score.

Tonight, Colby and I wrestle for the championship. The rest of the day, it's all I can do not to jump out of my skin.

"Stay within yourself," Coach keeps advising. This is his standard comment. Easier said than done.

Gary Hanson comes down from the stands and tells me he knows I'll be ready. "Jake's the guy I had to deal with all week," he tells the girl he's with. "Anybody sticks legs on Jake, he can get out. Believe it. Anybody." The girl gives him a dazzling smile he can't see. For a second I wonder why somebody so good-looking wants a blind boyfriend, then feel ashamed for thinking that.

Dad and Chopper show up. "Hungry?" Dad asks.

I am. We're allowed an extra pound the second day of wrestling, but I didn't eat much yesterday because the last thing I wanted was to miss weight at states. Today I'm too nervous to eat. My stomach's growling, but I can't stand the thought of a whole meal. Not yet.

Mainly, I spend the day watching Marcus. Now that he's dropped to the consolation bracket, he still has a chance at the bronze medal round if he wins twice more. It's an exhausting way to get there, but he's ready. He wins once, puts the Bad to the Bone shirt over his singlet, runs the cloth between his fingers. In the four years I've known him, I've never seen him so focused. When he wins again, Brian Fensel slaps him on the back and says, "You know how in the Olympics there was that ad that said you don't win the silver, you lose the gold? Well, the bronze you win. Go for it, Marcus."

Marcus lights up, as if it's just occurred to him that he could actually come out of this day a winner.

Coach has staked out a section of the stands where

we have a good view of almost all the mats. "Look," he tells us, pointing to the other side of the coliseum where the 189-pounder from Riverside is wrestling. "All four of our Maynard seniors made it to states, but only one made it from Riverside. And from the looks of it, he's about to get pinned."

Which is exactly what happens next. "I hope you noticed Coach Kimball laid low after regionals," Coach says. He never calls him Fuzzball. "Coach Kimball likes to talk big, but once his wrestlers didn't qualify for states, he got mighty quiet."

We consider this.

"Sometimes all you have to do is bide your time," Coach tells us. "You don't always need a big in-your-face kind of payback. It comes. It comes in its own sweet time." Coach leans back in his seat and looks as satisfied as if he's just eaten a plate of ribs and potatoes.

Some of the guys nod, but I don't. I think about The Mackerel in the principal's office and how just for a second her expression was exactly like Pole's used to be when he was about to get crunched. I think how much I enjoyed that. I think sometimes a big in-your-face-payback is just what you need.

Then Brian's words come back to me about not winning the silver but losing the gold. If I lose tonight, the one who'll get the big payback is Colby.

Not my idea of a good time.

The other guys wander off. Coach's voice comes at me from a million miles away. "I've watched you, Jake. Even while you were getting good, going to the top, you were already passing it on," he says. "I saw you try to cheer up Pole at regionals. Try to teach him a few things. That's a good quality, Jake."

I start to reply but my mouth has gone too dry to let me.

"Next year when you go to college at State— You could do a lot more good there as a handicapped student athlete with no scholarship than an elite one whose way is paved."

"I'm not handicapped," I say in a cotton-mouthed garble. Handicap is a state of mind. Handicap is relative. A truth I learned while Gary Hanson was turning my legs into braids of bone and muscle.

"That's just the point, Jake. That's what people need to know."

I run my tongue around the side of my cheek, try to lubricate it a little. "I'd just as soon stay anonymous."

"I sympathize, Jake. I do." He nods towards Fuzzball across the way. "Once somebody calls you a lying, cheating sack of shit in the daily paper, even if you're completely innocent, some people are going to wonder."

He scratches his bald head. "Some people, you can tell them a hundred times you don't have a problem as long as you take medicine, but they'll still think you're a freak." One thing about Coach, he tells it like it is. "But you can't hide from everybody," he says.

"I know." I think about Callie and Marcus, and how both of them turned out to be more trustworthy than I expected. I guess Coach has a point. I'm not going to make an announcement to the world like he's suggesting, but I guess I'm ready to reveal the startling truth on a need-to-know basis.

"You can't hide from your family," he says, counting on his fingers. "A couple of friends." More fingers.

"Maybe the girlfriend?"

"That's over." I don't say I was the one who ended it, or that I did it because I was afraid she'd start feeling sorry for me. Or at least that I'd never be sure. My next girl will know I'm Jake the Fits Man from the beginning, the way Gary's girl knew he was The Blind Guy. No secrets. From now on, what you see is what you get.

• • •

In the match for the bronze, with ten seconds to go in the last period, Marcus is up by one when his opponent doubles over and yells for injury time. The ref stops it.

"This guy isn't hurt, he's just resting," Coach tells Marcus. "All he's going to do is try to switch. Soon as the whistle blows, drive into him with all your might. A guy can't switch if you're doing one of those football drives you always wanted to learn."

The whistle blows and Marcus drives. He drives like he's been playing football all his life. And sure enough the guy tries to switch. And sure enough he can't.

And ten seconds later, Marcus has his hand raised in victory. The bronze. Third in the state.

He comes off the mat just as Coach rises from the coach's chair. Both of them open their arms. Marcus's skin gleams black with sweat but he isn't aware of it. He hugs Coach hard.

"Whenever they tell you what you can't do," Coach says as he hugs him back, "this is what you have to remember."

Marcus is crying. Tears make a translucent path down his cheeks. He doesn't care.

"You hear me?" Coach says. "Whenever they say

you can't do it, remember this."

"I will, Coach." Marcus gets control of himself. Awkwardly, he pulls away. Coach slaps him on the butt. As Marcus heads away, his eyes scan the stands.

He's looking for his mother.

Then Brunson grabs him and pounds him on the back. Brian Fensel and I give him the traditional high-fives. Marcus wipes away the tears and smiles wide. He stops looking for something that isn't there.

I think about Mom – who isn't here today either because she'd have to take off work. Who says she can't but really means *won't*. Who talked about needing money when she made The Big Career Move and later tried to make it sound like the job started as a matter of have-to and then surprised her. I don't buy any of that anymore.

I think Mom took the job because she was afraid. Afraid if she didn't grab a new life for herself, everything around her would move on and leave her there – me and Chopper especially. We're leaving her. It's true. Chopper's become a man with a nose on his face instead of a bump. Computerman with contact lenses and muscles. It's scary. And me – leaving things behind I never would have imagined.

And now Mom's leaving us, too.

No question, I would have liked her here today.

But like the woman said, normal changes.

• • •

"Have fun out there, Jake," Coach says before the finals. "This is really a no-lose situation. There's no worst. It's already a win."

What he means is, the worst I can do is get second.

Second in the state. Not bad. That's the worst. But like Brian says, you don't win the silver. I go up to the scoring table and it's all I can do to pronounce my name through my dry mouth. Too much is riding on this for me not to care. I'm a wreck. Sweating, but ice.

Which, when I think about it, is pretty normal.

I go out a little tight. Circle for a while. Take the first shot, but it's ill-advised. I get his leg but can't finish. He sprawls, fights me off. Counters it into a takedown. It's two to nothing, his favor. Next thing I know, he sticks his leg in, rides my legs forever and ever.

I do everything Coach said. Lower my hips. Sit. And – yes! Wheedle my way out with five seconds to go. First period ends with the score two to one, his favor.

Second period the coin flip goes to Colby, which means he gets to choose if he wants top position, bottom, or neutral. He defers till third period, leaving the choice to me. I take neutral. Circle, shoot, take him down. He powers into a standing position, tries to shake me loose. Can't. When I get him down again, he scooches away, tries to get out of bounds. Three times I pull him back. I'm looser now, feeling better. When second period ends, I'm up three to two.

Last period he takes the down position. All I have to do is hold him. But I don't. He doesn't just escape, he reverses me. I'm down four to three. He's got his legs in, and there's only a minute to go.

Instead of desperation, I feel completely calm.

A minute. It might be an eternity. I'm not in a hurry at all. I sit. Get his hips on the mat, step by step like I've been doing it forever. Work my right hand under his knee, grasp his heel with my left hand, try not to notice how he's jerking my face. There's nothing but me and him: sweat, concentration, a kind of focused heat. I feel when he's about to let go, feel him concede the escape. Jump up. The score is tied. I'm free.

No excuses now. This guy's trying to steal my dream. I'm in control here. A takedown wins this thing.

I give a little head fake, lower my hips. Sometimes you get a perfect setup. Not often. But now. I move forward – so flexible, so smooth, so fluid that I see what he's doing even before he does it, see him rock back on his heels like he's frozen in concrete, unable to sprawl because I'm flowing toward him like light. I'm flying; I'm electricity; I'm not even touching the mat. I know I have the takedown even before I have it.

Five seconds left on the clock. In one swift move I lift him, dump him to the mat. Put all my weight on him. After all those doors that have closed on me this season, I'm a heavy, heavy man.

Two seconds left, time in slow motion. I press harder; my mind floats free. Coach always says sports have no consequences and don't mean anything, but this does mean something, and it's not just about wrestling.

Like Coach says, it's about getting control.

I remember we're planning to go out for pizza after this is over. I remember how hungry I am. And by the time the buzzer sounds, all I'm thinking about is that extra cheese.

About the Authors

E.M. J. Benjamin is the pen name for a two-person writing team. One is a novelist with several popular books in print. The other is a high school wrestling coach who has sent many wrestlers to the state championships.

E. M. J. Benjamin's e-mail address is: emjbenjamin@hotmail.com.